Whatever You Want

A miscellaneous collection of writings

Sean Nicholson

FOR STEPHANIE

PREFACE

I can't recommend this book to you. Not out of some sort of false modesty. My writing moves me, makes me laugh, conjures images. Rather, it was not written for others. It is a complete self-indulgence.

If you are the sort of person to whom punctation matters, or the incorrect use of words is painful, then reading this will not be a pleasure. Mother you have been warned.

If you have got as far as reading this, I really hope you might keep going, but only if it gives you pleasure. It's a collection of random writings I did over the last couple of years. The theme is largely what I think when I sit in coffee shops. I find it a bit like painting; it takes my mind into a different part. A part where time goes at a different speed. A part where I can end up in unexpected places.

So please read it. If it gives you pleasure, then keep reading it. But be warned, it's self-indulgent, badly written, and I am not going to apologise for that.

Sean Nicholson
June 2019

THE SUN RULES IT ALL

The Sun rules it all. What I feel and see. The warming wind - tousling my hair as I look towards the sea - comes from the power of the sun pounding down on the earth. Boiling the air around me which rises, sucking in cooler sea air to fuel the wind. My feet burn as I walk on the ring of terracotta tiles around the swimming pool. I keep dipping my feet in the pool to create a layer of cooling water on the soles, like a sandal that evaporates in seconds and needs constant replacement. The smell is hot. I am Lawrence of Arabia transposed to the Sardinian coastline. Rather than an Arab turban and dress, I am loosely covered by shorts and a shirt with a single button done up. The warm wind rubs me all over like your hands when we are alone.

While the Sun rules it all, its army of power comes from its control of light. There is no subtlety outside. Everything is a solid colour, like some national flag. The sky and pool are blue. A deep, strong, powerful blue that lifts my soul while knowing I am powerless compared to its strength. Rectangular blocks of green lawn surround the pool. Specks of scarlet appear from the children's swimming costumes and the inflatable toys in the pool. After that everything is black and white. Pink skin looks white. The light-yellow wall opposite looks white. Chairs and sunshades are white. Little flecks of white cover the pool with reflections and splashes that show the water is alive. Everything else is black. The mathematical black shapes created on the ground by the sunshades. The sides of buildings cowering from the power of the sun. The army of little ants randomly searching for scraps of food across the tiles, oblivious of the power of the sun, or maybe even using it to power their clockwork legs.

"To me", "Sorry" – the children are laughing and calling to each other across the pool. They change in size as they jump out of the water then shrink back into it. There is no clock to tell them when to stop or start. The house with its Italian language books and television is no competition for splashing in the blue water. I climb the steps leading from the pool and garden below, to the house above. Ostensibly to get a refill of cold drink for recharge my empty plastic cup. The open patio door into the house looks like the entrance to an Egyptian tomb. The sun is raining down its best and brightest light on the wall around it, throwing everything inside the door into darkness. Its unable to compete with the sun. I pause ahead of the unseen then step inside and pause again. I have moved from a bold print to an oil painting. Shadows no longer have sharp edges. Shades of colour have appeared. It is like taking a kiln fired vase out of a square printed box. There are contours, graduations of colour, speckles, streaks and blemishes. The simplicity of the sun has become complexity as sunlight battles against this new world of texture and curves.

I look round half expecting to see you curled up on the cream sofa, but all I find is cushions scattered across it. No impressions to show you were recently sitting there. There is a half-read book left open on a page. You were here, but how long ago?

My plastic beaker goes down on the table. It was empty in the harsh light outside, but the softer glow inside means I can see drop of pineapple juice resting at the bottom. Leaving it I climb the stairs. If downstairs is a rich Victorian oil painting with furniture, wall art, and carpets, then upstairs is more like servants' quarters. Generous sized servants' quarters but lacking the wealth of objects that downstairs had on show. Bare white tiles, bare white walls, simple wooden doors. I open one.

The room is simple. A patio door is open to a small balcony. A light white linen curtain hangs down across the open doorway. It glows from the sunlight outside hitting it repeatedly with light. The wind outside is trying to get into the house, but the curtain is fighting back. Only a breeze gets past to fill the room. One end of the room has a tall light brown wardrobe. It does not look like it was ever a new wardrobe, rather it has always been given to someone who has no furniture of their own. The other end of the room has a small double bed with rumpled white sheets. If downstairs is an oil painting, upstairs is a watercolour of gentle blue grey shadows on white textured paper. The folds of the white curtain creating shadows on itself and the tiled floor. The pattern of the sheets like white sand dunes sculpted by the breeze. Then tucked amongst the sheets are light golden patches of you. The calf of a leg. A shoulder pushing up and out of the sheets. A river of hair across the pillow. A glimpse of a nipple like an oasis in the white desert.

I undo the buttons on my shirt and slide it off my back. My shorts fall apart easily landing on the floor. I have nothing else to take off so slide onto the bed. Your eyes open slightly and a second after the recognition in them a gentle smile occupies them looking back at me. I push a leg between yours. I wrap an arm around your waist and up your back. I weld your lips to mine. We start to make new shadows in the room creating our own light.

ALONE AGAIN

When I look in a mirror, I see the last member of my species. All around me are other species, going about their lives, communicating, touching, growing. None of them are my species. None of them understand me when I talk. None of them want to touch me. If they live or die it makes no difference to my day. I don't change what I wear or what I have for supper. I live outside a world of normal physics. Push me and nothing happens, there is no equal and opposite force back. There is nothing, just silence. I sit at my breakfast table with the sun coming through the window on to the tiled floor. If I am making a shadow from it, I can't see it, even my shadow is invisible to me. All around me are the signs of other people's lives. Leftover food wrappers, half read magazines, lost socks. People living at a different speed. They are the river, flowing, gushing, changing by the second. I am the rock in the middle. Immobile, inscrutable. They flow around me and sometimes over me, but never through me. They feel more in a second than I do in a day. I'm not even sure if they see me as their lives rush downstream. I am disconnected from everything with an out of body feeling from inside my head. If I reached out to touch this table and my hand passed through the wood, it would seem normal. As I look down to the blood flowing out of my wrist, it's more like a spilt glass of red wine than my life draining away. Blood is just plumbing after all. Does a house fall down and collapse because the pipes are burst? Yet a person becomes a body when their plumbing fails. I used to be a person, now I long to be a body. I want to take any final feeling away. Please numb my mind, and let my head become empty of these electrical impulses that keep the painful fire of thoughts alive. Thoughts are worse than cancer, unlike a tumour radiation goes through them and leaves them intact. How can something so intangible, so virtual, so non-existent, create so much pain. I can't amputate my thoughts. They seep back in. They teleport past any mental barrier. However fast I try to run away; they can run faster. Wherever I go they are in front, waiting for me, standing on every street corner, behind every door, under any bed I try to rest on. There are no peaceful moments, they can't stay quiet, more like a baby that never sleeps and is always hungry crying to be fed. My thoughts rain down in a torrential storm of small droplets that together flood and drown my mind. They create patterns in my head, patterns that look like him – his smile, his hair, his body, his eyes. Like a perfect storm they come together and trigger other senses. I can smell him as I breathe in. My fingers travel the sides of this chair as they travelled along his arms, feeling every hair, his warmth, his life. His life was my life; it was our life. Our world with plans for the future, what we would do, what we would become, how we would grow old together. A world and a future that was bigger than any sun. A sun that had exploded sucking the life out of him, and now me. A black hole that was sucking the blood from my wrist and will take the thoughts from my head. A black hole that was his poison and my cure. I want it to take both our souls so I can end my life with him in some parallel universe. Reunited in darkness.

The funeral was easy. It's a show for others. Funerals reflect cultures not emotions. Beliefs and values come to the surface for public display. They reflect the mourners as much as the soul eternally sleeping in the coffin. It's a time of decisions. What sort of coffin – oak, ash, willow. What about flowers – what colours, what types, what did the deceased like. The deceased suffered from hay fever and kept flowers out of the house. But the great thing about death is it also kills all the other diseases in the body it infects. We had a coffin covered in flowers and not a sneeze, or 'have you got a tissue' came from inside. It was a closed coffin. As it went past me, I wondered if he was really inside. He might really just be off on another business trip and possibly might call halfway through to ask me how I was and what I had done today. 'Sorry, I am at your funeral, can we talk later'. He didn't call.

They asked for some clothes to dress him in.

Pam, my mother in law, wanted him in that nice blue suit with the grey shirt and red tie. We had a silly argument about whether a body in a coffin should wear a tie. She seemed to think the occasion was analogous to a job interview. Maybe if you believe in an afterlife it is? That interview to review your life and see which part of the organisation might best use your talents. Neither he nor I are religious and that's how I won the day. He wore his red shirt that he would put on for a date night or a party. No tie. We got a 'celebrant' rather than a vicar or priest. It was a she, and she wanted to talk to me about his life so she could fully reflect his character. She didn't laugh until I had laughed once, but after that her voice was less hushed and I stopped wanting to scream at her to stop being so fucking polite.

The hardest decision was the music. You have 20 minutes from going in to going out. Allow 3 minutes for them to come in, and 3 more for them to get out. Then who do you want to speak. Allow 3 minutes for each of them. 3 minutes to sum up how you feel, what he meant to you. It's about one side of a sheet of paper. Is it okay to be selfish when picking the music? can I have my memories or do I have to shut them away in a drawer like underwear when people visit your house. Out of sight. Instead pick the music that says something to other people. The house that has been tidied up before guests arrive. I spent ages thinking about it, listening to old cd's of his, trying to find something that smelt of him. Then one day driving back from work a song came on the radio and I started crying as a drove. The memory of him, dancing with him at a friend's party, him looking at me, me enjoying being looked at, both of us knowing it was just the start of our evening, a dancing prologue to the coming symphony we would have that night. That was the song I wanted.

Everyone said it was a nice service. The men came in dark suits and ties. For so many men the formal wardrobe of business is also the wardrobe of death. Doesn't that disturb them. The women found hats and shoes from the back of their wardrobes. They asked subtle questions about dress code. They wanted to know the boundaries, what was acceptable, what was possible. It was sincere but it was also an event that demanded thought about outfits. You could map the relationships by who they arrived with. Families came together, all of them squeezed in a single car. Friends carpooled with their respective familiar faces. The university car, the work car, the Thursday night football team car. They all waited patiently outside like puddles of people. Small distances between each group. Smiling at each other, looking at the other puddles to see if they recognised a face they hadn't seen for years. The doors to the crematorium opened and the puddles started rolling downhill, coalescing to form a river of people entering the building. It was the same in reverse at the end. Doors opened, the river gushed out, but with less energy than going in, then the puddles of people began to form as they found their spaces. Before going in I was the one moving between puddles, shaking hands, accepting condolences, embracing those who wanted to embrace. I was a hostess more than a widow. Putting people at ease. For some outside the main social groups it was just knowing they were at the right funeral. For others it was recognising their attendance. Like any party there were quiet shy guests wanting to sneak by and excessively loud guests drawing eyes as they demonstrated their love for me. Coming out was different. I was the rock the river ran past. A toll booth collector taking their condolences once more as they went past.

We had a party afterwards. I could never bring myself to call it a wake. He would have preferred party to celebrate his life. Photos were taken to update albums, gossip and news was exchanged. Not much was said about him when people were away from me. It was a good party, people smiled, even I smiled. But there was no dancing. For dancing he would need to be there, so no dancing. At the end I paid the bill and went home to watch television. A numb contentment that I had done okay for him.

He died while I was making supper. For the last six days he had not eaten anything. His only liquid was me gently rubbing teaspoons of refreshing mango sorbet around his lips and mouth to moisten them. For the last two days not even that, he could no longer swallow and giving him a drink would have choked him. I had just put the potatoes on to boil. It was ironic to have started cooking for one before he had died. At this point he was easy to look after. No need for winches and slings to get him out of bed and lower him to the toilet or wheelchair. No need for prolonged meals, chopping up the food to fine pieces and drip feeding it into him mouth as he made a gesture of chewing then had to concentrate his mind to swallow it. No need to find conversation about lives that he was no longer a part of. No need to read out his post and make a pretence of asking him what he wanted to reply. I still dressed for him, and did my hair the way he liked, just in case he opened his eyes for a few minutes. His bed was in the dining room. He had stopped going upstairs to our bed a month and a half ago. Maybe that's when you become a widow – when your partner can't make it up the stairs to share your bed. The dining table had gone, in its place against the wall was a bed that could go up, down, raise his legs – probably do the ironing if I could work out which buttons to push. I had a small desk in the other corner to use my laptop while keeping him company. The distractions used to be looking for holidays we could go on, now they were looking at old digital photo albums reminding me of who we once were. When he was more awake, I would turn to him with lines like "remember that villa near Toulouse with the cat" or "wouldn't you love to go back to Tobago". He would gamely make a slight grimace of a smile to show he had heard and was up for it once he got better.

I never knew if he realised he was dying. At the start it was unspoken, and towards the end unspeakable. We only mentioned it twice during the entire nine months of the reverse pregnancy. A medical diagnosis leading to a death rather than a birth. There ought to be a word for the period when you are terminally ill. Unlike a pregnancy the time seems so indeterminate. No doctor likes discussing time, because unlike a pregnancy a terminal illness leaves the doctor looking like an amateur. If you push them, they talk about broad timelines, 'a few months maybe'. It was the opposite with my first pregnancy. The doctor smiled and after doing some calculation gave me an estimated date for the birth. Not a year or a month, but an actual date you could plan your life around. She told me, that if the baby came late, they could induce me to help ensure we stuck to the plan. With a terminal illness no one wants the date to arrive. It seems that with so many other factors at play, a due date is not possible. It makes it so hard to plan. Planning to have the kids out of the house or planning a date for the funeral that fits in with other people's lives and does not clash with national sporting events and already booked summer holidays. A year before all this we had taken an annuity out for his mother. I was struck by how honest a process it was. You tell them about yourself and they calculate how long they expect you to live for. Then they give you a price. I would have liked to have taken him to see them and got an expected date. Without a date you don't know when to discuss things like what sort of funeral might he want, and to share your most personal thoughts and gratitude for sharing his life with me. You can never share your anger for him leaving you. How selfish it is that he chooses to die and leave me alone. That he was going to break the marriage contract. You might swear till death do us part, but when I said it, I was thinking my death not his.

The first time it was mentioned was when we were waiting in a hospital corridor. Posters on the wall warning you to check yourself, avoid too much alcohol and asking for blood. We laughed about the last one because who wants blood from someone already in hospital. If I have a transfusion he said, I want it from someone as far from a hospital as possible. Maybe a Sherpa in Nepal halfway up an ascent of Everest carrying some Europeans rucksack for them. We were waiting to see the consultant. I say, 'the consultant', in reality there were so many we saw that I should rather say 'a consultant' not 'the consultant', but it is always 'the consultant'. The brain tumour had been diagnosed and the question was whether surgery was possible. The consultant would decide. 'If he says no, we should go out to supper and make a list of what we need to sort out before I die' he said with a serious smile. I told him not to be morbid, and not to prejudge the outcome. The consultant said yes, so we never had that dinner. He told us it was risky and there was no guarantee of success, but we just smiled and said we understood because we both knew the alternative was certain death. The night before the surgery was the second time. We had made love, not saying it but knowing it might be the for last time. Not elegant or passionate love, rather familiar and slightly forced. Holding me with his warm breath on my neck he told me to find a new partner if it went wrong. Not his permission. More his wish to me to let him go in peace. Of course, I said that was silly, the operation would work. Then he cried gently into my arms and shoulder saying, 'I don't want to die'. The surgery did not go well. They removed most of the tumour but not all of it, but in the process messed up his brain so he was unable to walk. Overnight he changed who he was. We never made love again.

In all the time after the operation we never discussed his dying. We couldn't. He had turned overnight from the partner I planned life with to another child I had to look after. There are things you don't discuss with your child even if you are do the planning for them. No one who visits wants to discuss it. There are lots of 'how are we today'. Friends were great, they would come over and we would sit in the dining room chatting in ear shot of his sleeping or awake body. Often, we didn't know which, but I told people to assume that he could hear us, and that he enjoyed listening. I think he did. On bad days he would shout that it was terrible, and that he wanted to die. As if he did not realise that he was going to. He never said I want to die faster, just I want to die. After a while as he got frailer and less aware. The cries to die stopped. I don't think it was an acceptance or awareness, rather the reverse an unawareness, more like a pet who just lives in the moment rather than future or past. I could never ask if he knew he was dying, if there was anything he wanted to tell me. Did he enjoy being married to me? Had I been a good wife? What were the best moments for him? I still don't know the answers.

I wasn't even sure he was dead at first. The line between sleeping and death seems a slim one. I stared at him looking for a sign of movement, listening for a noise. For weeks it had been like this. I would come into the room wondering if he was still alive. Looking for a sign. There always was, though it might take up to a minute to find it. I stopped worrying and understood that people are both tougher and more fragile than I had first believed. Five minutes passed with nothing. Three minutes past six in the evening. I had already been given the leaflet on what to do when a relative dies. I picked up the phone and started dialling.

Do you know you might be dying? I don't think so until someone tells you, and maybe not even straight away then. For a few months he had been getting tired and unable to do long physical exertion. We both put it down to a new job and the arrival of autumn, taking out the energy that you get from a summer day. Then he started to mention a numbness. It would appear in part of an arm, or a leg, then disappear. That's normal isn't it? We were getting old; he would have turned fifty in two years. We expected things like this. Even after we went to visit his friend from university who had been diagnosed with bowel cancer the thought never crossed our minds. We sat chatting to the frail friend, much of his hair lost. A cheerful black humour from his side, a concerned 'here to help' from our side. On the drive back we agreed how tough it must be. We touched wood that it would never happen to us, at least not until we were over ninety. Never did we think that death was with us sitting on the back seat listening to our conversation, waiting to cast his shadow.

The first worrying sign was the partial paralysis. His leg started to drag a little, and he reported the side of his mouth seemed to be stuck. I thought it must have been a stroke. It had all the signs, impacting one half of his body. I was worried but it was not death. Strokes were things that could be lived through. I could be supportive. We could change our diet. If it was really bad, he could use the bus more and if that didn't work, I could drive him. But none of that hardship would change us. Our world, our plans, our love. I still had a vision of our future; Chatting over a cup of tea about our day, weekends away on the coast. I certainly didn't imagine myself alone with the cup of tea, no one to ask how I felt.

The doctor started with 'the most likely things'. It made sense and reassured us. I believe now it is the wrong approach. I met a risk analyser at a party who explained to me that probability alone is the way to make mistakes. It should be probability and impact. A one percent chance of dying is more important to check out than a ten percent chance of getting a cold. Start with the brain scan, then move to check the circulation. I know you can't go around checking possible disasters all the time, it would drive you crazy. Going into the doctor and him saying 'let us first rule out a brain tumour' would just spread terror and paranoia. But was he thinking that? As he pumped up the blood pressure cuff, was he secretly think brain tumour, or just what he would have for lunch. I can't forgive the doctor for either thought. I don't think I can forgive any of the doctors and surgeons who were so helpful, so concerned, so professional but who did not save my man. They showed us the brain scan with a large white lump the size of a satsuma in the middle of the head. They cruelly told us that had it been smaller they could have tried radio therapy but since it had grown this big that was no longer an option. Some said how impressed they were that he was still able to walk with a tumour that size in his head – I said he was a fighter but started to realise he was the walking dead. The oncologists met with the surgeons and told us it was a long shot that might buy more time. Like some rescue mission to save trapped miners underground they showed us where they would burrow down through the skull and between the left and right hemispheres to reach the tumour. I could imagine it as a report on the late-night news, covering the story with diagrams and interviews with experts explaining the risky nature of it. We never hesitated in saying yes to it. No one was offering us anything else.

We were married on an autumn day with bright blue sky and a cold wind. No morning suit and wedding dress. I had a cream skirt and top with little bits of lace and a swirl to the skirt as I turned. When buying it I imagined myself dancing in it more than walking down an aisle. He decided the formality required him to wear a jacket, but to make a point he also wore a bright tie with pink elephants on it and kept pointing to it talking about the elephants in the room. The only proper invitations were to our parents, everyone else had a 'if you are free please join us at the registry office', and about twenty of them did. We already had the house, the joint bank account, the dog. It was a wedding to cement and celebrate rather than bring two people together. Looking at the photographs there are faces of people I had forgotten were there. Some faces I still see today but with different hair styles. Some faces that have gone and are just occasional images on web pages I come across. In a years' time I would become pregnant and while we never said it to each other, getting married was also the starting gun for a family. I knew I wanted him as the father for my children. He was kind, patient and generous. I hoped they would look into his eyes and see the same warmth and gentleness that I did every time.

We decided to honeymoon first and have a party once we were back. It was our way of getting married, low hassle, focus on the sociable fun rather than the formality and expectation. That's why we were so good together. We felt the same way about life, what was important, what didn't matter and what could be left to happen by chance. I don't think I talked to him for more than ten minutes at that party. We had our photos taken together, we cut the cake together and we danced together. I talked to friends and relatives knowing he was in the room doing the same thing. Knowing that we would both go home together at the end of the night. I don't believe in soul mates or people who make you complete. I do believe in someone who makes me happy, who calms me when I am around them, who hurts me when I don't get enough attention from him and who understands me. A person who can cheer me up with their conversation, warms me with his eyes and the touch of his fingers, and I can run to when I want to hide.

Of course, I slept with him on our second date. I don't approve of that and would think my daughter silly if she did, but it seemed so natural and quite the logical thing to do. How could I not sleep with him? It never crossed my mind for a second that I would not; all I thought was would he want me? It was like Alice down the rabbit hole seeing a cake with 'Eat me' written on it. Looking at him I knew that taking a bite would be both indulgent and change me for the better. I could see how generous his lips looked as he talked to me about something, I have no recollection of. The way his upper lip slightly curved would surely fit perfectly with my lips and I so wanted to find out if it did – it did. His eyebrows reminding me of my uncle who had entertained me as a child and taught me to ride a bike and helped me, with endless patience, to pass my driving test. When he touched me, the world stood still for an instance as I felt the ripples move through my body. A massive surge of self-awareness would wash over me, not self-consciousness in an embarrassed way, more like an out of body experience studying the change in blood flow through my body. Then he would look into my eyes and I would become weightless. My senses would stop and just focus on him. No more wind on my skin, no more pressure from the chair I was on, my breathing would pause, and I would fall slowly forward. I don't undress easily in public, my skirts are longer rather than shorter, yet undressing with him watching was easier and more natural than being alone. I wanted to give myself to him, and I did.

On our first date we talked, and talked, and talked. My sister said I had to meet him. He would be perfect for me. I said she was mad and that no blind date could possibly go right. She made fun of my failed love life, trying to embarrass me into submission. Of course, she brought up the man with the foot fetish, and the month with the body builder who tried to convert me to weight lifting. 'You really have no idea about men, and I think as your sister I am a far better judge of who you should go out with'. She was married by then and desperate to convert me to a couple who could join her for holidays or suppers, rather than be the odd person who threw everything off balance. After whipping me into submission she changed to showing me the carrot with a photo on her phone. Not a great photo but enough that I gave in. It didn't show his eyes and there was little character to him. I only agreed if there was an exit strategy. My sister had to phone me after thirty minutes with an urgent message. She said it should be an hour, and we settled on forty minutes. She even booked the restaurant and the man. All I had to do was turn up – but not dressed like that she said.

I sat in the car outside the restaurant wondering why I was there. Did I really want or need a man in my life? What were the chances it would be this one? Could I imagine meeting someone, falling head over heels in love with them, marrying, building a life together, feeling safe and complete, growing old together even after we had told each other everything we had to say. Could I really believe there was a man somewhere who could make me feel good about myself after years dipping in and out of depression. Depression often caused by my relationships and self-doubt. Was love possible that could remove all that burden and create more sunshine than cloud. I wanted to believe it was possible. I locked the car and walked across the car park wondering what I looked like and hoping he would already be there. The restaurant was busy and as I waited for someone to seat me, I scanned the chairs. He was sitting in a green jacket and playing with the knife and fork on the table. Other people sitting alone were hiding in their phones, but he was clearly part of the world and happy in himself. Gentle self-confidence. As I was taken across to his table, he suddenly became aware of my approach and looked up at me, straight in my eye. No embarrassment, just curiosity. I felt a slight ripple in my body but kept walking. He stood up. Taller than me. His hand reached out to politely shake mine. Another ripple went through me.

"Hi, I'm Peter"

GRITS

    I'm waiting for an order of 'grits'. I am not sure what grits are. Where I come from grit is the small sharp stones you put on a road to fight back against skidding on sheets of ice. Grit is what you give birds that swallow it to accumulate in their gizzard, so they can grind down seeds into edible food. If this is the price of having a vegetarian diet, then I am out – and it brings new meaning to the phrase getting stoned. But I am not where I come from. I am in New Orleans, US of A. I know from the movies that real men possess grit. It's a determination possibly bordering on stubborn stupidity. It's what makes our hero charge down against unassailable odds and makes us feel proud of them while they act so foolishly. It keeps them climbing the rock face to safety when their arm is broken, and blood is pouring from a gash on their forehead.

    A young man in an apron has just brought my order. In front of me is a plain china bowl containing a creamy white particulate mash. Maybe the similarity with small sharp stones is closer than I thought. I want to tell them that serving white food in a white bowl makes it look less appetising. A slight horror of tasting this is starting to form. Images from years of badly made school porridge and mash potato are coming into my head. Adults are telling me to eat it all even though it makes me feel ill. Will this be a regression to my childhood? Am an adult now and able to leave it if I don't like it?

I dip my fork in tentatively, the same way I test the water temperature when I swim. It's a gluttonous mass. It moves but holds together. Millions of fans at a rock concert all separate but joined by the occasion into a jelly like a super organism. It touches my tongue. I would like to tell you that I was pleasantly surprised, but I can't. A wave of initial revulsion. Have I misjudged it with my advance negative prejudice? I look out the window and chew praying to the heavens to find some pleasure. My eyes lock with another pair. Long brown hair and feminine eyelashes. The 'free ATM' machine between us blocks the rest of her face and body. She could be in a bourka since her eyes are all I see. I realise I have new pressures. I don't want to grimace with such appealing eyes looking at me. Will I ever become an adult and be able to eat as I wish, express my true feelings openly and not feel judged. She walks into the café and becomes a normal person rather than a woman of mystery and consequential creator of macho self-pressure. I swallow and immediately reach for a gulp of my coffee. What is it, and who voluntarily eats it? Is it called grits because you need true grit to eat it? Someone must like it. It's on lots of menus. It can't only be ignorant people like me who order it as a failed experiment in widening their diet.

I look around the café to see what others are eating. To my right two women are meeting for their Saturday morning brunch to catch-up on their week. One if talking while also holding and tapping at her phone. The other sits cross legged talking animatedly like a Buddhist on caffeine. They have plates of food but no grits. I decide grits are not the next dietary craze that health conscious city women will embrace. My table is by a closed window. On the other side of the unclean glass are two older men. They clearly arrived separately. I don't think know each other but have started up a conversation. Unlike the two women they have their bodies facing away from each other, ready to close up the conversation if they feel uncomfortable. Both have grizzled beards that could be a lifestyle choice or just laziness. They are not looking to impress women with their choice of clothing. They have come to pass time. If anyone would be eating grits, I figure its them. One of them could even be described as gritty. Times have changed, they both have latte coffee.

So where does that leave my thoughts. I think grits must be today what porridge was ten years ago. A lapsed food no longer a necessity, and not yet rediscovered. They are waiting for someone to come along and make them trendy again. They need a journalist to call them a superfood, or a TV chef to demonstrate new ways to eat them with chorizo and coriander. I still don't know what they are made of. Is it a special seed or bean? If it is and you are a farmer my advice if grow chilies. If you are a stock market investor, stick to pork or orange juice markets. But if you are an aspiring TV chef, this is the opportunity you have been looking for. You will know you have succeeded when you see me ordering brunch and saying, 'I'll have grits with that'.

SLEEP WITH HIM

They say Pride comes before a fall; I say it comes before a lonely night in a bed on my own. Don't get me wrong I have pride and I think it's good to have pride. I also have an empty bed, well apart from myself and Jeremey. Jeremey is the most loyal man/bear in my life. He has stuck with me through school, puberty, university and two boyfriends who both laughed at him. Jeremey understands all my thoughts like no boy or girlfriend can. He reassures me when I need it, and provides familiarity with his warm, yet lifeless, eyes. For all his great features that I would want of any future partner for life – not the lifeless eyes – he is not able to make me feel loved in the way a man holding me can. This was a severe disappointment I discovered, first at 13 when I realised the poster on my bedroom wall did things to my body that Jeremey never had. I am too ashamed now to admit to who the poster was of, but if I tune into a Channel 5 game show late at night a shudder goes down my spine as I realise what a near miss I had escaped from. You need to understand that we would have married had I managed to find a way for him to meet me. I had no doubt of that at 13. At 19 I discovered he had publicly announced he was gay. I think that's why I broke up with Sam.

Sam was my first tangible love. Unlike the poster on the wall, I could smell Sam, see him from the side and back, hold his hand, and for the first time I had a relationship where the eyes could move and follow me, bliss. Of course, with reality like this came problems. Now that my boyfriend had movable eyes, I found they wandered. They wandered to TV sets with football, they wandered to girls in the street. They wandered up and down my body at times when I was talking. I sort of liked that, but at the same time it was irritating if I was trying to be serious and explain my newfound socialist views that would make the world a more equal place. I don't yet understand the balance between having a man look at my body in lust, which sometimes I like and sometimes just disgusts me. It's the same body, I am the same person, the looks are the same. Sam put it a little more succinctly. "Make your mind up, do you want me to look at your tits or not" he said in a slightly irritated voice one day after I asked him to focus on my face so he could better understand why vegetarianism was better for the planet. It was shortly after this that I realised his eyes also wandered to young men in the street. He started working out a little more and wearing tighter t-shirts. For a while I was very happy with this. I had standards I expected from any man I was going to be seen with, and envy from other women was one of them. We would regularly have long kissing sessions, but I was cautious, and he was not pushy. I took this to be a sign that somewhere underneath his baseball cap there was a gentleman waiting to appear and start holding doors open for me. Having known more men since Sam, I realise this was unlikely. The day that I read about my first, two-dimensional poster lover, announcing he was gay, was the day I broke up with Sam. I still had the poster in my bedroom, looking down like a smiling Stalin. Sam was sitting on the end of my bed. Jeremey had been consigned to a corner chair to watch like a psychiatrist watching a couple in counselling. Sam turned to face me. I looked at his brown eyes, then at the brown eyes in the poster. I looked at Sam's black hair, and then the black hair in the poster. I glanced between the tight t-shirt in the poster and the tighter t-shirt on Sam. Then I just blurted out "Are you gay?"

A relationship with a young man can't recover from a question like that. I don't yet know if any man can take that question and still carry on in the same relationship. Which is weird because most women could no problem. Some might even consider it a compliment. I am not sure if that's because it's harder to see woman making love to a woman as a form of rape – where's the penetration, the invasion of the body when a penis is not involved? Could I claim to have been raped by a well-developed tongue action between my thighs? I have never heard a man expressing positive curiosity about his sex with his own gender. You don't often hear men describing their male friends as handsome or beautiful, but women do it all the time when talking about their friends. I have had numerous complaints from ex boyfriends about my habit of describing many of my friends as beautiful. We would enter a room to introduce my latest boyfriend to a lifelong beautiful friend. The boyfriend would enter like a dog looking for a bone, clearly thinking some Marilyn Monroe figure would be about to enter their life. It must be some measure of how hot your girlfriend is based on how hot her friends are, the male dream not just being to go out with an underwear model but that all her friends would be underwear models too. I know from experience the pressure of such a friendship would is unbearable. More than once I experienced it with my friend Katharine. We would be in some sophisticated bar, all retro lighting, mirror walled toilets and mojitos. A walking bottle of testosterone would approach us looking for a way in. "What do you lovely ladies do?" the hopeful Romeo would ask. "I'm an underwear model" Katherine would reply in her jeans and jumper, then I would add "And I'm an environmental consultant" in my low cut red TopShop dress. Being a man, it took a second or two to process these two bits of information, then I would see the eyes swivel and his shoulder and side re-angle to block me out. I tried various approaches to deal with this. Initially I would go for sarcasm and logic. "Really?" I would say "I spend my day saving this planet, making it a better place for future generations!". Then his voice, recognising the wisdom and beauty in my argument would rotate his back even further towards me and ask Katherine "Do you have any pictures of your work?". My next theory was I had to go one better than underwear model. On one occasion I boldly replied, "I'm a porn actress". For some reason he did not question this, and it worked like a charm at first, but it rapidly became difficult to sustain. He asked what films I had been in. Please don't think of me as a prude but I don't know the names of any porn films so had to make them up.

"Debbie visits Leamington Spa, Big Breasts go wild in Brighton, and Nuns on Holiday".

He seemed to accept it but after a moment's thought said, "But you don't have big breasts?".

"CGI, you can do anything with computers these days" and he nodded wisely. Being on a roll I added, "and I got an award for that film".

Irritatingly rather than just be impressed he asked what the award was for, I ask you, can you name the categories of awards for porn films.

Katherine who was smirking behind him blurted out "Best scene with a goat".

He thought again "How do you have sex with a goat?"

"It's easy because they are horny"

Please don't judge me but later in the evening I did go home with him. I did fancy him a little, mainly because he fancied me and for once I was the focus of attention rather than Katherine. At this point I realised that being an underwear model they just expect you to have a nice body, but they expect more from a porn actress. He kept asking me to "do some porn stuff". I mean really what do men expect a porn actress to do that an environmental consultant would not do, it's insulting really. Inspiration came to me with a memory from a Cosmo guide to 7 ways to blow your man's mind. I can't remember what number it was, but one of them suggested using a series of small indeterminate words like "There, yes, lower, yes, now, more". This worked surprisingly well at the start, in fact he clearly responded to it, but then I got stuck for words and kept accidently dropping in words that actually came into my head like "No" and "Really?". This confused the poor chap and made me realise that it takes more than I thought to be a porn actress. Clearly porn actress is above PE Teacher for any career discussion.

He was the only one night stand I have had. Of course, I mean so far in my life. I like the phrase 'so far in my life', it suggests there is much more to come and most of it will be better. I bit like saying of your weekly lottery ticket 'so far in my life I have only won ten pounds'. The implication is clearly there that I expect to, and shall, win more than ten pounds. It has so much future potential and is the opposite of my father asking, 'what are you doing with your life?', which sounds like so much of my life has passed away never to be recovered. Death could strike at any moment seems to be the implication from my father. At that point I will be judged and found wanting. St Peter standing at the Pearly gates to heaven will ask for my name and start to scan through his big book, repeating my name to keep it present until he finds my life history laid out in it. He will pause then look up and earnestly ask 'Did you really spend that much time on Facebook?' to which I will reply, with a tear in my eye, 'I thought I was going to get more time'.

I am determined to do more life and less Facebook. I want a life where St Peter has to first turn over at least two pages before asking 'How did you fit so much in?'. Hence my underwear dilemma. I have agreed to meet Daniel for a date. Becky showed me a series of photos of him on her phone. If I was Becky's husband, I might have been offended by the way she slid her finger across Daniels's face to move from photo to photo. Caressing his wide mouth with generous lips. His photo didn't even blink when her finger poked his green eyes with their playfulness expression tinged with tenderness. She ruffled his black hair that looked like it would last at least until after our second child.

"He's just out of a relationship, perfect for you"

"Who broke up with who?"

This matters of course. What I was really asking was why is he single now.

"I don't know but he is not going to stay single for long. I casually showed him some photos of what we did last weekend and he asked who you were"

Well that of course sealed it. I will go out with

any man who looks at a group photo and asks who I am. It's like being in the fruit bowl and having someone pick you rather than the other tangerines and apples. I looked less bruised, more radiant, and the potential to create a wonderful first bite with juice running down his chin.

Here's my dilemma. On a blind date with a gorgeous looking man, should I plan for possible passion, admitting to my baser desires. Or go unprepared, to represent my higher moral values. It's the eternal dilemma of the white dress or the red dress. Flat shoes or high heels. Underwear or lingerie. Condoms or paracetamol. I don't like admitting to myself I may be planning to seduce or be seduced. It should just happen, like the weather, but should I go out without an umbrella if I am thinking of rain.

Why can't we be more like Birds of Paradise. David Attenborough was on the other night explaining the various ways they select a mate. It made Tinder look primitive, no swipe left or right. There was jumping, stepping, shaking, even hanging upside down. And the best bit was that the men had to do it all. They had to worry if their feathers were shiny enough, did they look fat with a purple tail. The women were drab as could be and completely in command. A group of male birds would dance around on two branches they had somehow selected from an entire forest of branches. After a bit the female would turn up, probably just back from her manicure. She would look the men up and down a bit which would drive them into a frenzy of the male bird equivalent of twerking. Then without so much as a conversation about star signs she would point her feathered finger at one of them and off they would go into the forest. No question of morality, no worries that other birds would call her a slut, no asking if he would still respect her in the morning. She was way cooler than that. If women were called birds because of this I would sign up today, and just think of the time and money she saved compared to me.

I've gone for my green Debenhams bra and pants. Green is more decent than black or red. It's the sort of colour underwear you could wear to a social event like Ascot or Henley. If I get run over and the ambulance comes, no one's going to look at green underwear and making a knowing look to their colleague. In reverse green is still a powerful statement, and it does match my eyes. Any man who works this out should be devastated by such colour coordination – to date none have worked it out. Just to be clear it's not some sort of pastel green, this is a full on, traffic light, you are clear to proceed green. I don't want any mixed messages after the problem with Simon. We hadn't made it to my bedroom. Instead we were decorating the carpet bit by bit with each other's clothes. I was indulging myself by lying back having told him I was his and he could do as he wished. To be honest his wishes were quite traditional, but it was still exciting stuff, but a bit like a computer game he seemed to be stuck unable to move to the next level. His fingers were running up and down the sides of my legs, his lips were creating a contour map of my neck, and no area of my chest seemed unexplored. His head then moved down my body and was kissing my left hip. The magazines all said it was good to help a man know what you want so I decided a little encouragement was needed. My right hand stoked the side of his face and started to apply a gentle horizontal pressure. I assumed this along with his moist lips for lubrication would easily slide downhill to reach the desired location. As my hand pushed his head pushed back. A memory of Mr Smythe trying to teach Physics came into my head. For every force there is an equal and opposite force. I had never really believed this was a piece of information I was going to need when I was older, but it seemed it extended as far as the laws of love making. I pushed his head a little harder causing his ear to bend slightly. The ear, and with it the rest of his head pushed back even harder and suddenly my arm gave in – I am the weaker sex – and his head went flying away from my body and hit the corner of the sofa "Ow".

The combination of memories of Mr Smythe and Simon's shout of pain had poured cold water on my personal fire.

"What were you doing?" a slightly flustered Simon asked straightening his tousled hair.

What was the correct lady like way to explain my action? "I was just trying to encourage you to explore a little more. You know… all parts of me want attention."

"What about your pants?"

"Yes, that's the bit that was asking"

"Well it's a bit of a mixed message. I do wish you could be a bit clearer"

"I thought pushing your head towards them was pretty unmistakable"

"What about the writing?"

"What writing?"

"You pants say 'Keep out, private property' on them"

I looked down. They even had a picture of a little locked padlock on them. I never got to consummate with Simon, but when people ask how many men I have slept with, I say five and a half, and Simon is the half.

So tonight, there was no humorous writing on my underwear. Next was the jeans or dress choice. Jeans made it seem more informal and not to boast but I could win Guildford rear of the year when I wear my black stretch jeans that had shrunk a little. However, the dress was more feminine, and I wanted a masculine man. I slipped the dress on and looked in the mirror. I slipped it off – not good for my legs after the bruise I got the other day falling off the bicycle while trying to follow another cyclist up on to a pavement short cut. So my red dress with the V back? No, red V backs and green bra straps don't work. I had a sudden thought, what if he was colour blind? Would he think my red dress was green, or my green underwear was red? Not that I expected him to see my underwear, but should I be undressed it would be embarrassing to ask if he liked my green underwear if he thought it was red. I chose my flouncy flower dress. It made a statement that I was confident, but that I was in control. I decided to start the evening with a single button undone at the top. If it was going well after the starters, I would release a second button while nipping out to the bathroom. Maybe a third after pudding?

London transport is very socialist. There is none of the class distinction you get on mainline trains with first or second class. Pessimists think they are slumming it in cattle class with the unwashed masses. Optimists think they have been upgraded to first and might be rubbing shoulders with the rich and famous. If it's a busy tube train then rubbing shoulders, elbows, bum and potentially hard rucksack with sharp bits pointing out. I don't know of anyone who looks good on the underground. The long tunnels and escalators with cold fluorescent lights that can turn an Essex girl with a tan to snow white. Stairs to remind me about the decision I made to wear high heels. An apparently blind busker singing 'Love is all around us'. Sudden winds along the platform as trains arrive and depart causing my hair to behave like seaweed being pulled by a strong tide.

I boarded a circle line train heading east. Depending on the lighting and whereabouts in the tunnel we were, I would catch glimpses of my reflection in the window opposite. In between self-inspection

I read the adverts along the top of the carriage for teeth whitening, employment agencies and a musical based on the life of Donald Trump. A change of train line and one hundred and twenty stairs later, I stepped out into the night air outside Covent Garden station. The normal mix of people waiting to meet friends was hanging about the entrance, along with a man thrusting leaflets that were modern day treasure maps explaining the route to find the best Indian curry in London. Nowhere on the leaflet did it say where Daniel my date was. I got my phone out and search for the WhatsApp message from Becky that had his photo in it. Its only when you have to search through your WhatsApp conversation threads that you realise how much rubbish we say to each other. I got past the evening where she was cooking Stroganoff and kept asking for help, how many ounces to a gram, is it okay to use self-raising flour to thicken since she was out of plain flour, why is it called Stroganoff – was there ever a Mr Stroganoff who created it, the Hungarian equivalent of the Earl of Sandwich. I found the photo, studied it, then looked around the crowd of people in the streetlight and shadows. I realised now there were things I had not asked about Daniel that I should have. Firstly, I had no idea how tall he was. As I scanned the crowd I prayed for a negative result as my eyes moved down to a face, and a positive result once my eyes moved above my level. Secondly, was he intelligent or stupid? Obviously that's doesn't matter when looking at a photo and deciding whether to risk a date, but when half the people in the crowd have hats, scarfs or worse hoods, up around their face you start to think could he be that stupid as to hide his face when waiting for someone he has never met. I made a mental note that in fact this was a good ploy to use on a real blind date. That way I could check out the man while still hiding in plain sight. For five second it was a brilliant dating tactic. On the sixth second, I thought 'but if we both do it then it will be chaos'. A sort of Prisoners Dilemma situation – that's for those of you who read popular science books. And yes, just because I go on blind dates and worry about my underwear does not mean I don't read books or watch Brian Cox documentaries on the TV!

There was a man against a wall with a hat on, but no scarf or hood, who might be Daniel. I looked at him, without staring but enough to indicate my attention. Like trying to get a man in a night club to come and say hello. He was intently looking at his phone – this of course is one of the problems of modern life. Trying to catch someone's eye is so much harder than in Jane Austen's day when people were so bored they looked at everything. I thought about lobbing a small stone at him, as people do in films to get others to come to a window. I realised of course it was silly. I could just go and ask. Part of me was attracted by the idea and if only I had worn pumps rather than high heels – no ability to run away afterwards. I started edging the phone with its picture of Daniel up. If I could hold it up to compare the 2D photo with the 3D person I felt sure I could answer the identity question. But how to do it without attracting attention to myself and appearing more of a hitman checking his target before pulling the trigger. Modern culture came to my rescue. Reaching into my handbag I found the selfie stick that Becky and I had taken to the Take That concert last year. I slotted my phone in and held it out in front towards the man with the hat. To maintain the idea I was just taking a selfie, a normally quite socially acceptable thing to do in public, I adjusted my hair and pouted a little. All the time looking at the screen then darting across to the person. Same nose, same hair – but different eyebrows. Do men pluck their eyebrows and change their shape. I didn't know of any that did. It felt like the same as asking if there was a male equivalent of a Brazilian.

My phone suddenly went ping very loudly. The man at the wall looked up which made me look down in my surprise. Even in that millisecond I realised if really was not him. My phone meanwhile was trying to tell me something. It came from a number that was not in my address book. It said, "Running late – Daniel x". Was a kiss really the right way to sign off. We had never met in person and here he was x'ing me at the end of a message. I started to reply saying Ok but got stuck. Should I put an x at the end as well? It seemed rude not to – a bit like when someone says I love you and just replying thank you. But if I did sign off with an x what would it mean? I went with no x. I have standards. I started to wonder how he got my number, but the phone went Bing again and it said, "Got your number from Becky". Clearly a mind reader. I wondered where he was, and once more as I thought it the phone went Bing like some mind reading genie – "just walking across Covent Garden square from the Strand". I turned around and walked to the end of the street that opened out to the square. The normal assortment of Covent Garden street artists was on display. I guess they only go home when the tourists go back to their hotels. The immobile man covered in metal paint, waiting to surprise a passer-by. A failed X factor contestant was singing 'Walking back to happiness' in front of a large suitcase with a few coins in it.

Further on I could see people entering the square from the Strand. Like particles of smoke they came through the gap and then started to drift in different directions. Which one was Daniel? My phone went ping again – 'in a red jumper'. He was a woman's dream, able to read minds and answer questions before they were asked. A red jumper was striding across. Not walking, this man was striding. With purpose. I texted back 'found you' and a second later, with no pause in his stride, the red jumper looked at his phone and looked up. I waved. He saw it immediately. No hesitation, no fumbling, he waved straight back. I started walking towards him. I didn't want to run even though somehow, I had the urge to turn the meeting into a slow-motion scene. He had just gone past the busker when the mood changed. The busker threw down his guitar and shouted, "Stop Police". I first heard it as "Stop Please" which shows you what a silly thing it is for the police to shout. Daniel turned to look behind him. As if waiting for Daniel to look away the metal immobile busker jumped off his wooden box and started running towards Daniel. Daniel had started to turn his stride into a run but seeing the metal man bearing down like some Terminator from the future he changed direction. The singing busker launched himself at Daniel and caught his arm. Holding tight to the red jumper whose arm was getting longer as Daniel struggled. The metal man arrived and knocked him to the ground. Other passers buy started to stop and watch. Daniel was on the ground and I could hear shouts of "I'm innocent" while metal man produced handcuffs and proceeded to arrest the innocent Daniel. They pulled him up to his feet and started marching him away as he turned to look at me. Not knowing what to do I waved. A Chinese gentleman watching the whole scene put his hand in his pocket, walked up to the busker's suitcase and dropped some coins into it.

When asked how many men I have slept with I now say five and three quarters. I think had I met Daniel he would have asked to see my green underwear, and I would have let him, so it should count as a quarter.

THE ATTACK

"Don't go near it" the mother screamed pivoting her pram of precious cargo away and urging the eight-year-old girl to return to safety. The girl stood still in awe as the danger carried on approaching. She is transfixed. Mother is saying this is a danger to avoid, but her eyes are telling her it's a thing of beauty and wonder.

"Come here now" the urgent scream that you hear in the park from parents and dog walkers. Implacably the danger kept moving forward, foot by foot, its rear end moving from side to side like a slow horizontal pendulum. A pendulum of death so great Edger Allen Poe dared not write about it. A danger that has traumatised adults for years, and as I could see now mum was desperately trying to pass this fear on to future generations. So dangerous she was not able to move forward and recuse her girl for fear that both of them may be attacked. Or was it the inability to easily anchor the pram? The dilemma between letting go of the pram which may roll to an uncertain fate, or save her daughter from a certain fate? This is where pram manufacturers have missed out and failed to understand their customer. At some point every parent has the emergency while pushing the pram. For some parents it happens many times a day, but of course they have naughty children so maybe that is evolution selecting for well-behaved older children who never stray from the pram. Just as the escalator has the emergency button to stop it, the car has the air bag, so prams should have an emergency brake activated by high pitched parental screams. Instead mum is wrestling with a foot lever, the diaper bag has got caught up and is stopping the lever from moving. The baby inside is awaking to the fact that mum is stressed and is starting to cry in sympathy – yes, it's always the parent's fault how we turn out. And through all of this, the waddling danger is getting closer, and taller, seeing a stationary eight-year-old girl as a source of today's lunch.

The wise reader, which must be everyone who reads this, is probably asking by now, why I, the author, am not rescuing the small girl. The simple answer is "do you think I am mad; I know how much danger she is in!". Thanks to my parent's advice; well screams and pulling me by my arm away from perceived dangers, I was now an adult wise in the dangers around me. I am wondering if I should offer to hold the pram. That way I can protect myself but appear sympathetic. I know in today's world this could make things worse. Every adult is a potential kidnapper and child molester. My offer could add a third danger to the two mum was already trying to choose between. Did I mention I am a man?

Well based on the circumstances so far you may not think me a man, but at least I am male and human. Or put another way I am a man, but we could debate if 'I am a Man'. Why is it people always assume it is always men who are the creepy kidnappers and paedophiles? Women just trust women automatically. Children are warned about talking to strange men, teenage girls talk about creepy men, even men make jokes about sick men. But never women. My teenage daughter never talks about the creepy woman who followed her home with two Waitrose bags of shopping and shoes that did not match her dress. Put a man in white socks near a school and he would be arrested in seconds.

I am a Man, so action was needed. I spring panther like towards the mother.

"Excuse me I think your daughter goes to the same pre-school as my son"

She stopped for a second, foot tangled in nappy bag, and looked at me. The baby decided to follow and stopped crying and also looked at me. Even the eight-year-old turned to look at me.

I continued presenting my credentials.

"I think we met at Amber Walkers birthday party. You brought the coleslaw and gave me a wet wipe to remove chocolate cake from my Jake's face"

Awareness was spreading across her face and I pushed home to close the potential friendship.

"It was very nice coleslaw; I especially liked the pineapple chunks in it"

"Oh, hello again"

We had established I was not a potential third threat and as a mutual parent it was okay to scream in front of me at her child.

"Lucy come here now!" she tried to stamp her foot to emphasis the command but the nappy bag just broke open and a bottle of talcum powder fell out. The pressure of the fall was too much for a pound shop product and the lid came off. A nuclear mushroom cloud of white talc covered the mother and baby. The baby smiled. Lucy laughed. Mother whispered "Shit". Lucy smiled again "You said Shit". Mother paused to reflect on her life while others looked on at her playing the role of white-faced clown in the park.

Alas Lucy having realised that I was not only no threat, but a parent, reverted her gaze to the white monster she was in awe of. By now two other mothers had rescued their children and were dragging them away. Their talk was of lunchtime, ice cream and parking tickets that were about to run out. Their children were asking if it could really kill you and could they have a flake in the ice cream. This left Lucy all alone like a lone pine tree with an approaching forest fire.

"Can I help and hold your pram while you get Lucy?"

I asked this trying to sound deep in my voice, masculine in action but with a sympathetic feminine side indicating that I would get Lucy, but the mother and daughter bond is so much stronger and hence effective in a situation like this where every second counts. She looked at me once more and then offered the pram handle. I took it and she moved towards Lucy.

Like all mums she was a fast learner and always looking for advice from others. Her voice relaxed a little moving the desperation to the back of her throat, like a child hiding under the sheets when the monster is beneath the bed.

"Lucy dear we have to go, its lunchtime"

"We need to go now our parking is about to run out"

"If we go now, we can pick up some ice cream on the way home"

Lucy suddenly understood; this was a bargaining situation. She was thinking for a second and knew what she wanted.

"Can Natasha come around to play?"

Mum paused. I knew why. Natasha was fun. Fun if you are an eight-year-old. Fun if you have a maid in your house to clean up afterwards. Fun is you want your child to learn new things and new words. I could see that mum did not have a maid and decided repeating shit was enough vocabulary for one day. But mothers sacrifice for their children. They might complain about their husband's friends and say they don't want to see them. For their children's friends it has to be subtler or you just have to throw yourself on the sword – maybe it should be, throw yourself on the Dyson.

"I think Natasha is busy today"

"No, she said her mum and dad have gone away"

It made so much sense, Natasha's parent clearly had a maid and a nanny. They might be paid, or they might be grandparents but either way I understood how Natasha had become the A-list party invite she was. The Paris Hilton of the pre-school. She probably has an agent to manage her birthday party appearances and Mothercare endorsements.

"I don't think she will be allowed out if her parents are away"

"She went to Bethany's house yesterday"

"How do you know?"

"Facebook."

I looked at the mother with I hoped my sympathetic expression. The Internet had ruined being a parent, undermining our authority, overwhelming us with blogs from other perfect parents, and becoming a new source of parental concern. In my day parents worried about evil words if you played a vinyl record backwards. I never even worked out how to play my records backwards, and I am certain my parents were not able to, yet they believed it was a possible source of immorality. The Internet had made that seem so negligible. Like access to an older sibling's bedroom in a disapproved neighbours house, the internet had porn under the bed, Nazi posters on the wall and explained the best way to use drugs.

We had reached that moment where everyone knows the dice was about to be rolled, in a few seconds everything would be immutable. Safety or death. Lucy did not know this but her eight-year-old mind was weighing up choices. The large white monster had reached striking distance, its red mouth opened as a small black eye weighed up the situation. The white-faced baby clown in the pram was our audience looking from face to face for a clue as to whether she should feel happy or sad, and hoping for another cloud of talc to explode everywhere. I looked at the mother. She looked older, the talc had coloured her hair grey and made her skin pale – I hoped there were no mirror or shop windows on her way home. She looked to the sky for a second and then inspiration hit. She was going to win.

"He's getting ready to bite you" she said more matter of fact than urgent. She reached into her bag and without looking at Lucy calmly spoke.

"I'll just get a plaster ready, and my phone in case we need to call an ambulance"

The gods were with her, a gentle hiss came out from the red mouth of the monster. Lucy looked up and realised not only did it hiss but it was bigger than her. She looked at the plaster in her mother's hand. She had a plaster last week after the fall off the wall. She didn't like having to get a plaster, it meant she would be in pain.

"Just throw it on the floor and walk slowly back to me. Don't turn and run or he will chase you"

For a second, I admired the mother but then started thinking why was the monster a he? The mother was a she, Lucy was a she, judging by her clothes the baby was a she. The only he around was me. So why did the monster have to be the same gender. Did calling it a 'he' make it scarier than a 'she'? From my experience she's were much scarier. Had literature taught this mother nothing – Snow White, Hansel and Gretel, Sleeping Beauty. Children had more to fear from evil women. Evil men are too busy trying to kill adults because their focus is more short term. It's your evil women who think ahead and deal with a threat before it grows up.

Lucy decided. Her hand raised, then jerked forward, opened up to release and scatter the bread from her hand onto the grass in front of her. She turned and walked to her mother. Her mother turned to the pram and we swapped looks.

"Thank you" she said.

The baby in the pram smiled and they walked away. I turned to look at the monster who had also won. The swan was reaching forward to claim its prize of a bread lunch.

THE BREAKUP

It was character assassination made to look like putting your grizzled hair Labrador out of his misery. The slight watery blear in the eyes made more visible by sitting outside. The normality of sitting in a park. The cruelty of it being a park where we had walked hand in hand, arms around waists, legs walking in time enabling us to meet lips and walk. I had kissed her while her back was arched against that cherry tree. The same tree I could see now behind her. When you put a dog down it's a calm conversation in a well-lit room. In the past you would have been discussing toenails that need clipping, or booster injections to prevent kennel cough. When discussing quality of life, it's the same room, the same people. All that change is the tone of voice. So it was with us. She had the skinny jeans and green semi combat jacket my fingers knew so well. I knew their texture; I knew the easy way to undo the buttons who were familiar friends. She had first introduced my fingers to them. Her tone had changed, like the vet. The difference being it was about her quality of life not mine. As if the vet was about to commit suicide and wanted to rationally explain it first. When we put our dog down, I remember smiling out of polite agreement as the expert gave his view. I read about a Soviet dissident who was arrested by the secret police and the retrospective shock he felt from the fact he had smiled and quietly gone along with his own arrest, not quite believing he would end in prison. I was the same with her break up of us.

I couldn't really understand and kept waiting for the real reason. She talked about things like incompatibility. The evidence list included my house and how I kept it. We always met at her house, so this seemed like citing the moon is made of cheese as a reason – impossible to understand why it was relevant. The focus moved to the feeling I was not driven, I wanted to experience life but not drive it. More of a passenger. She wanted a driver. Her mad ex-husband who tortured her was cited as at least having the virtue of believing he should be prime minister and could cure everything if only they allowed him to. Really - Everything but not his marriage. Was I talking to a hidden Eva Braun who was only just starting to reveal her true self? For every problem there was a compliment. Imagine a stick of rock with intertwined red incompatibilities and white compliments. A stick with my name running through all of it. There were no questions. No seeking to understand or clarify if the statements were correct. The goal was to break the stick of rock in half. One half of us didn't want to fight for 'us', the other half still didn't not understand what to fight against. It was personality racism. You don't say you are black, rather you disagree with the culture of being black. She said something about me not having a suit and worries about her friends not liking me and my friends getting on with her. I was the wrong sort of boyfriend for her life.

All this time I take it like an idiot. I hold her hand. I smile sympathetically. I see her as a child with a bag of hand grenades and golden teddy bears. They are all being thrown out while she looks for the meaning of her life. I try to catch some, shield her from others that I miss. I have been here before. It's been a circular path to get here. The previous emails asking what our relationship means. An insecurity at times of distance that would disappear in seconds once we meet. This time it started when we met. This time my face is the trigger. I shaved my beard off as a surprise for her. The gift I planned becomes a sign that this change for a new life is destined. It's tea leaf reading logic, and she is a believer. I don't know if it's real or temporary. Based on statistics the relationship may still be fixable, but this is a new step. An hour before sending me the text asking to meet, she had been with her therapist. She's a surfer and this is a big wave the therapist helped her get on. Holding her hand while she balanced on the board and waited for the wave to carry her and her message of death to me. Will I eventually be the beach she lands on or the rocks she needs to avoid?

Just to be clear here. I have been a bad boyfriend over the summer. On more than one significant occasion I have placed my worry for my children over my wish to be with her at an important moment in her life. Don't read that as altruistic or kind. It's a conscious decision to value something higher than this relationship and that's not good for the relationship. It's like mixing bits of sand with petrol and hoping the car can still work. She is the warrior willing to charge down the hill and asking me to come with her. I have been the cautious one preferring a more guerrilla warfare approach than outright fight to take on the world with this relationship. We are on the same road, but she is in a sports car and I am in a used saloon car not always managing to keep up. Together is wonderful but there has been too much being apart.

She asks for time apart to think. God knows who really believes that. I don't. Relationships are solved by communication not introspection. You don't see United Nation negotiators asking warlords and dictators to go off and think what they really feel and want. I put this down to lack of self-awareness on her part. As we walk back to the car park, hand in hand, I am still trying to understand. She reaches up on tip toes and kisses me affectionately. I have no idea why and kiss her forehead the same way I kiss my eighty-year-old mother. The sadness and anger that will grow during my evening are starting to wisp into my mind. I leave quickly. I don't look back. I don't run. I just walk with my head down still confused.

By evening I have more anger. There is a battle in my head. One side wants to scream at her for being so judgmental and shallow. For no longer loving me for what I am but rather focusing on what she wants me to become. I am an adorable puppy that she has chosen to trade in, rather than spend the time with it at puppy training. Or is it just aesthetic – does she think a Jack Russel would suit her lifestyle better than a Retriever. Work better with her home, her clothes, her friends. Why hasn't she asked me what my I want, whether there are ways we can make it work. Where is the commitment to making relationships work rather than the consumable approach to replace rather than repair? I force the anger down to let other better thoughts share the oxygen in my mind. She does have periods of insecurity; this may be one of them. If it is, how can I help her, what does she need to know or see? Do I trust her self-awareness – she has difficulty focusing and like the surfer can be buffeted by waves and wind into unintended directions. I build a theory. Partly out of logic and partly out of hope, because I have yet to accept the reasons she gives me. If I accept the reasons then not only is she right, but also, she is a disappointment to me which could be worse. I construct a theory around my changing work life, the fact I have not discussed it enough with her so may have miscommunicated thoughts I find trivial but that matter to her and what she sees as a possible future. I don't know if it's a theory build of straw, twigs or brick. Is the change in my life that I feel confident and relaxed about, causing waves in her life? Is this just a case of misdiagnosis? Rather than needing our relationship to die, does it just need better communication as the medicine to cure it?

The next day the anger within me has started erupting with frustration. It drives me to start dismantling and removing things round my house. A need to take apart and change things driven by an inability to understand and take action against the real problem. Throwing away bits of metal and cooking gadgets I now see as stupid decisions. Objects acting as surrogates for memories of us I am discarding. My phone rattles on the table. It's a message from her. She will miss me. Who calls to say they will miss someone? I find some rock music to put on loudly and carry on throwing parts of my past life into piles ready for the dump. I could sell the house and move. I could go online and create a new account on a dating web site. To the question 'what sort of person are you looking for?' I would reply a sane one who can communicate! I don't start doing either because deep down I still have hope. I realise that I still think she loves me but just doesn't know it. My denial phase. I try a message to her phone. I keep it simple. I am in pain and I don't understand. No more than that. No ask to meet or talk. I don't think I could face her. The thought has been going through my head for a day that I could not make love to her. I could not even just have sex with her. I suspect any erection would be more like a rolled-up newspaper after an hour in heavy rain. I still love her but the anger with her is so overwhelming it freezes any ardour. My phone buzzes. The message says she is missing my lips and my gentleness. She is just not sure I am right for her. We are so different.

I feel vindicated. She does love me in the present. It's the future that is the problem. Worse she is right. I have difficulty imagining the future. We both have baggage and ropes keeping us where we started this relationship from. Neither of us can jump off the cliff embraced in each other's arms. We are not that selfish or insecure. Not to ourselves and not to the people we love and who love us. It's our own Romeo and Juliette but much more mundane, life goes on regardless. Sometimes it's a disappointment that we don't all go around killing ourselves for love. Thank god we don't. Even with her change of position my anger does not subside. It's still driving me. Making me walk in circles around whatever room I am in with my mind going in even faster circles. A whirlpool of anger that my soul is caught up in. Unable to swim free, strong enough not to drown.

WHY DO YOU LOVE ME?

I was being asked the question directly. We were suspended in each other's arms. Sheets had been ruffled and creased. Passion had been spent. Love had been declared, but now the question was why. It is easy to tell each other that you love them when your blood is pumping through your body, and you're recovering the breath that you lost in physical love making. This was mental love now. This was demonstration of love to feed the mind and soul for the dark hours and days ahead of when we had to be apart. Maybe it was also to reassure us that the previous time had been well spent. A request to show the foundations that our declarations of love were built on. A fear that the words could evaporate, as clothes went back on and phones were checked in preparation to leave, the bubble of love.

It's not an easy question to answer, at least not easy without some thinking and rehearsal. I don't mind declaring my love, but I see so much risk in explaining my love. I might pick the short straw to talk about and offend their view of themselves.

I don't yet know what they think of themselves. Do they like their body? No one likes all of their body. Which bit don't they like? Are they embarrassed by their legs but proud of their face? I once dated someone who thought their feet were too big. They would never wear sandals or flip flops for fear people would stare. It's no safer to talk about their clothes. Admire their jacket that they borrowed at the last minute from a friend with better clothing sense.

I find it safer to talk about something more ethereal. Their style, their character. I want to be honest. Honestly, I have no idea why I love you. Can you really analyse love? Would a lawyer in a court of law be able to convince a jury that I love you? If they did, it would be by my actions, giving gifts, sending messages, holding hands, kissing. I can show that I love you. I can't show you why I love you. Really, I think you should go first and tell me why you love me. Give me some clues as the right way to do this because I have no idea.

A small voice inside me is asking if I can't explain why, then how do I know I do love you? Could my love just be a correlation. An emotional coincidence whenever I see you. Without a why, there is no credible basis for our love. It's a tabloid headline. Once you read the full article you discover that it is not what they really said. There is no logic or evidence. Rather someone said, 'maybe I love you' or 'it might be love'. Possibly an expert in love was asked to comment. 'it has all the signs of love, but until we can kill it and perform an autopsy, we can't be sure'. You can't shine a light on a shadow to see it better, but a shadow is still a real thing. Could love be the same?

Suddenly it all changes. I have been looking at this all wrong. Why am I so stupid? It is not a question with a logical, physical, tangible answer. It's about how I feel when I with her. The answer isn't about them, it's about me.

"I feel happy with you. Safe, warm. Your love feeds my love. I like how I feel when I see your smile. The feeling I get as your eyes look back at mine. I love you because as I go about my day you come into my thoughts in a hundred different ways. Things I want to show you, things to discuss with you, stories I want to tell you. The anticipation in my body as I walk down your street getting ready to knock on your door. Feeling alive when you touch me. Upset when you fail to notice some small change in me. Pride when we are out together. Lust when I see you undressing and getting dressed. The feeling I have that life is better with you than without you. That's why I love you."

COFFEE SHOP

I was going to write about the perfect woman... don't all rush at once to tell me it too hard, or there is no such thing. There is such a thing, but now is not the time to tell you about it. Why? Because there is a harder and more controversial topic. What is the perfect coffee shop? I spend a lot of time in coffee shops. My children say I spend too much money in coffee shops. Adverts often say ' for the price of your daily cup of coffee' to suggest affordability. If you have a daily cup of coffee, then we are talking about one thousand pounds a year. Imagine I offer you a thousand pounds. Would you tell me 'you know what, I am going to buy a coffee every day for a year with this generous gift'. Of course not. That would be madness. If you are a man, you would get a TV that requires three men to move it and doors to be taken off hinges to get it into you house. If a woman, then forget practical, you would get 'seriously' impractical green shoes, with skyscraper heels, golden tassels and a guarantee to make your best friend jealous. You might even place all of the money on red and let the wheel determine your fate, but never, never, would you say let's buy three hundred and sixty-five cups of medium skinny latte.

That makes me a coffee shop investor. More than one percent of my disposable income goes on coffee shops. The United Kingdom funding for overseas development aid is less than one percent. Governments aspire to spend two percent of their funds on defence. If I was a government, my spending on coffee would exceed my overseas aid and defence spending. I would need to have a Minster of Coffee to oversee the Ministry of Coffee. There would be national coffee policy. After public consultation civil servants working on the national coffee policy would introduce coffee legislation, disperse the coffee development fund, respond to coffee questions from members of parliament. Luckily my government is extremely efficient. I am Minister, Ministry and Civil Service all rolled into one. Our meetings are very efficient because of this. There is no splinter group arguing that Colombian beans are unethical. No demonstrations advocating for a caffeine tax to stop the impact of late-night coffee drinking on the national economy. I am the government, the opposition, the voice of society. So, you would think with all this unanimity there would be nothing left to discuss on the perfect coffee shop. Alas no.

Think of the number of variables. Location, ambience, service, furniture, wall art, queue time, clientele, space, music. That's not even thinking about the coffee, blend, cup, temperature, milk choices, barista showmanship, surface pattern, sugar choices. Let's not even mention food. Now take all the combinations of choices and add in my, or your, character. Angry, happy, tired, anxious, soulful, sociable, unsociable, sick, ebullient. Needles in haystacks have been found faster than the perfect coffee shop. Men and women in search of soul mates have found them, married them, and divorced them in less time. You could win the national lottery multiple times before solving this problem. Why would you even try to solve it?

The reality is I have never tried to solve it. Rather it is a journey, a search, a quest. Statisticians will tell you it is a quest that over time can only get worse, not better. They are right. How many coffee shops are there in the world? Too many. Imagine you visited a new coffee shop every day for 50 years, that's eighteen thousand two hundred and fifty coffee shops. There must be more coffee shops in the world than that, so the bad news is you can't visit all the coffee shops in the world to be certain you have found the best one. It gets worse. Every time you visit a new coffee shop, is one less time you can go back to your favourite coffee shop. What is the point of having a favourite if you can't visit it regularly? It just becomes your favourite memory of a coffee shop.

Memories are the video photo album of my past. I flick through them. Pages sometimes stick together. I can't always remember where and when some of them were made. Wisent Josephine with me then, I can't see her in the memory, but I am sure she was there. As I turn the pages of my coffee shop memories I smile with recognition. I frown from lack of recognition. I have well-thumbed pages I linger over. I skip over other pages faster when finding a memory I would rather have lost. It's a video album that is always changing. I always think the children have been playing with it when I was out of the room. Some memories are missing but come back at a later date. The order changes all the time. Chronological order is not a phrase that can be used. Any use of the word order fails. It like a multidimensional game of musical chairs with the lights off. I get to light a match when the music stops, then five seconds later the flame goes out and the music starts again.

The perfect coffee shop must be staffed by baristas. Not because they make better coffee, rather because they are better showmen and women. Japan has its tea ceremony. Amazon tribes have the preparation of the hallucinogenic drink. I have the barista seduction. That is the seduction of me by the barista. It is a asexual seduction. It's the look they give you acknowledging not just my existence, but the fact their day has been made so much better by seeing me. It's the way they repeat my order with a reverence that acknowledges the brilliance of my selection. Latte, one shot, skimmed milk - their eyes say brilliant how did you think of such a great combination. For them none of this 'could you wait a minute'. I get a 'coming right up!'. They understand how important my time is. Some just can't help themselves 'What name shall I put on the cup?' they say with a marker pen poised to take my dictation. I muse on 'Ferdinand the second', 'Baron Thistle-whistle', 'Bond, James Bond', but settle for 'Frank'. They repeat it like a wine taster - 'Frank..' as they roll my name round their mouth to fully savour the beauty of it. Sometimes I get a 'My favourite uncle was called Frank'. It shows we are probably related. I am potentially family for them. It's wonderful, until I hear the next person in the queue ordering and being told what a brilliant choice they made. Its wasn't love, it was just seduction.

Music is like lipstick. Get it right or don't do it. Classical music is wrong. I am not here to die or looking for an environment that supports working on advanced mathematics. Pop music is too friv-olous. It makes the shop similar to a duck billed platypus - a ludicrous collection of incompatible features that make no sense. Yes, it exists, but it's not evidence of a higher life at work. On a single occasion I encountered heavy metal. Nothing in a coffee shop should be made of heavy metal. It is akin to serving my latte in a uranium mug. The playlist for me is a mix of African, Mediterranean and Latin – and I do not mean Gregorian chants in Latin They are all music with life, energy and soul-ful warmth. Better yet I don't understand any of the words. I can't sing along. They soothe me but are unable to distract me. There is one exception. On a Sunday morning retro pop music is allowed. But only before midday.

Clientele determine ambience. A lack of them is a problem, as is too many of them. You should never have to compete for a table. I have been in queue where advanced mathematical modelling is happening in my heads. There is one free table, but two groups ahead of me. Should I be ordering in a takeaway mug, or just solve the problem by taking myself away before making the irreversible commitment of ordering. A scanning of the customers shows over a half have finished their drinks, but only a tenth look like they might be ready to move. Afterall a coffee shop is a place of meeting, not a place for coffee. There is a mother with two restless children. They have finished their milkshakes, taken the last biscuit crumb, and are now focused on throwing paper serviettes at each other. She is the opposite of a racing driver. She wants as long a pit stop as possible before getting back in the race. How long before her children drive her away? Before, or after, I wander between the tables with my latte? Beside her is a row of laptop loungers. In later years these same people will occupy rows of deckchairs on seaside promenades. They are in it for the long run. They are forming relationships with their table and chair. Some may even have their post redirected to the coffee shop. My favourites are the retired couples. They come in for a tea. They discuss the quality of tea, the weather and Maud's bad hip. Once the cups are drained, they will announce to each other that 'it's time', and they leave. These are predictable people, and I am grateful for them.

The best coffee shops bring your drink to you. They take the pressure off. They mentally massage my shoulders. They invite me to relax and be their guest. There is nothing better than hearing "we will bring it over". Spoons, metal flags, pyramids. I have been given them all. Each with a unique number to indicate my order. My pride at being given number one. Concern at receiving number thirteen. Communication is a two-way thing, so I ensure my number is positioned facing the kitchen with its regular departure of servers carrying trays of food and drink. I need to avoid the terror of seeing a member of staff carrying my order in search of number 7 then at a loss returning with it to the kitchen.

Once seated my clientele needs change. Of course, the loud family, child, man on a phone is a problem to avoid. There are subtler problems. The intriguing customer. The person who has something, is does something, saying something that distracts me. It can me more distracting than cat videos on YouTube. You can pause, rewind and stare at a cat video. In a coffee shop you need to cast furtive glances. Find reasons to turn round and put a face to the voice, without appearing rude. I once spent a frustrating twenty minutes trying to read some writing that made up a large tattoo. Its owner was a 'hairy biker' who I felt unable to stare at directly. My solution was a silver flowerpot. It mirror like qualities were excellent. The fact it was curved was not so helpful. It magnified and shrunk the tattoo. Worse still, all the writing was back to front. To this day I still don't know if he was announcing his love of Mother or Murder.

In a #metoo era can I admit to being distracted by women in coffee shops? Will I be ostracised as a pervert or rewarded for my honesty? That decision will rest with you. Be kind. It is the intrigue I long for. A woman I can only partially see. Partially hidden by a plant. A leg extending from behind a room divider. A husky voice behind me. These one-way encounters can make a coffee shop memorable. One such assignation was with the Caffeine Chemist. She had long black hair, a taste for chunky wool with an off the shoulder look. Gracing a tall stool by the window where sunlight gave a glow to her outline. Possibly an angel, but not. No angel would have a delicate pink bra strap showing. All that was beautiful. What made it exquisite was her drink choice. She had a coffee and a coke with a straw. I would have ordered one then maybe the other. This lady committed up front to the caffeine, hot and cold. She was embracing her commitment to the morning. An open laptop in front of her revealed she was reading about structures of benzoic compounds. Something I know more than the average man about, but less than her. An angel with a passion for life and polycyclic hydrocarbons, could she be real? Not wishing to spoil the moment I left without ever seeing her face but stealing the memory.

Inoculations, insurance, and Wi-Fi in coffee shops. I find them all necessary for my life, but I wish I didn't. Wi-Fi can make the social become anti-social, the quiet become noisy, the relaxed become stressed. Teenagers giggle and make wild gestures as they compare smartphone screens. Men, occasionally women, glue their eyes to a laptop screen giving nothing back to the humanity in the room. Road warriors interrogate baristas on Wi-Fi passwords 'Is that lower case or upper case?', 'One the word or one the number?'.

Wi-Fi passwords tell you a lot about an establishment. If you need to ask for the password, they are not focused on me. If the password is designed to be secure with upper, lower, numeric and punctuation characters then they have things other than customer service on their mind. Ease of use is no excuse for lack of imagination. The name of the establishment, or the town it is in, is a sure sign of practical furniture and passive wall art. They are not about the experience. Quirky, humorous, memorable. These are the signs of a good coffee shop. 'CoffeNotWar', 'AnotherCup?', 'BeanHere'. Once I had to type in 'ILoveYou', and yes, I felt loved.

Coffee shops have replaced communal facilities like laundrettes and tea rooms. They are where we meet, greet and take a seat. A neighbour once told me 'I now only meet in coffee shops because my house is so untidy'. Little did he know I judged him as much by the coffee shop he chose, as I would have by the state of his sitting room. By nature, I am a punctual person. 'Let's meet at ten thirty' means I arrive before ten thirty. With great punctuality comes great responsibility. I normally select the table we will be sitting at. Not too close to the ever opening and closing door with people man-oeuvring prams and shaking wet umbrellas. Avoid-ing tables near the counter where people loiter and queue casting shadows and disrupting natural equi-libriums of our conversation. A window is good for light and to reassure my guest they have the right coffee shop as they wave to me from outside on ar-rival. Finding each other is not always so easy. Some shops have multiple floors and multiple rooms. A few have courtyards that must be crossed by brave souls. Having watched elite forces storm an em-bassy I know the drill. Moving from room to room I enter, scan the faces, mentally say 'Clear!' and move on to the next room.

Punctual people face the problem of when to order. You may be able to enter a coffee shop and just sit at a table waiting. I cannot. I feel the weight of responsibility to be a customer not a visitor. If I have no coffee or cake in front of me, no number flag indicating I am waiting for the kitchen to deliver then I feel like a table parasite. Occasionally I an-nounce in a louder than normal voice to the barista 'Just waiting for my friend to arrive', hoping every-one understand I will buy something, and to make clear I have a friend. Forsaking this I often order on arrival which creates its own problems. Inevitably my friend will arrive five minutes later and inevit-ably I feel compelled to offer to buy them a coffee. It's a stupid offer, they might say yes. Yes means I have to leave them and my coffee. They keep my drink company while it goes untouched and gets cold. It's like leaving a prostitute with a well-behaved bishop while I go to the cash point. Such a waste of everybody's time.

Unlike chatting on the internet, coffee shop conversation is neither listened to by security services, nor recorded for posterity to be quoted back to you ten years later. Privacy however is not guaranteed. A good coffee shop is not like a Paris restaurant. You need space between the tables to ensure that when you lower your voice to discuss indiscretions, eyebrows are not raised at neighbouring tables. Clearly some conversations are so boring privacy is not an issue. Listening to a discussion of Gladys wrinkled skin condition is not only instantly forgettable but also puts me off my carrot cake. Similarly, hoteliers swapping stories of sheet cleaning challenges will ensure I avoid pastries with streaks of white icing drizzled across them.

There comes a time when the coffee mug just has dried brown stains coating its sides. Holding it gives no warmth. The small plate just has the walnuts removed with care because I only wanted coffee cake. Paper napkins have been wiped across lips and crumpled up. Smartphones have been doubled checked for messages requiring immediate response. Watches are showing that parking tickets have five minutes left before risking imprisonment. Chairs are pushed back. Coats put on, and eyes scan for forgotten possessions that might forgetfully be left behind. I weave through the tables, even raise a

'Thank You' to the staff for letting me visit and pay them money. A pull of the door and cool fresh air washes over my face. I look left and right, pull up my collar, and step out in search of my next coffee shop.

Dog's Life

The man going past me at speed is being pulled along. His outstretched arm is not offering to shake hands with me, rather it's like a magnetic compass, continuously changing direction as it is attracted to the large hound in front of it. There is a line that joins them. Traditionally we call it 'a dog lead'. The implication is normally that we lead the dog. A dog lead is for taking a dog for a walk. Yet at times it could be interpreted as 'a dog lead'; the case where it is the dog that is leading. The scene is more reminiscent of one of those trials of strength competitions which I would watch muscled bare backed young farm works perform at agricultural fairs. They would have a large tractor tyre attached to them via a rope. Their job was then to race against other similarly encumbered, testosterone filled competitors. Today it was the dog that was racing, and as a test of its strength, someone had put a human at the end of the rope to slow him down. The fountain of green vegetation at the end of the road would seem to be the finishing line. A local park. No doubt full of other like-minded dogs all waiting to see who can bark loudest, run in circles fastest, and destroy sticks with the crunchiest sounds of their teeth gnashing.

The man being led smiled at me as he sailed past. I think he was trying to suggest he had a level of control. It failed because just as his eyes met mine, they suddenly were yanked away and all that was left was an empty space with an accompanying 'owww' sound as if a plaster had been suddenly ripped off his hairy leg. His four-legged companion had seen a cat and was keen that his 'master' join him in following it. The pair shrunk as they accelerated off into the distance. I knew we would meet again. I was the tortoise to their hare. I also was heading for the local park, and it wasn't a large enough park to lose a dog that large in.

My arrival at the gates of the park was much like my arrival at an event I have been told to network at by my boss. My goal would be to get in the room without being seen. This is not what is expected of me or hoped for by my management. If already in the room and they see me a arrive then a sudden bellow of my name and excessive waving of hands would destroy my dream that someone might have invented networking for people who like to stay invisible. I know there are many others like me. I even considered a Tinder like networking app to help. The goal of it being to avoid having to talk about oneself. Rather than a photograph of yourself with list of interests it would consist of a series of 'If I was a .... I would be ...". For example, rather than a photo of yourself you would have to pick a Disney cartoon character that best reflects you. This would be followed by a series of questions with drop down lists of answers. If you were a month of the year you would be ..., If you were a country in the world you would be... You get the idea. Questions like 'If you were a car you would be...' would not be allowed since they are clearly too competitive. Only categories where there is no one answer is better than another answer would be allowed, 'If you were a letter of the alphabet you would be ...' This way there would be no loss of ego. You could look at other profile and not feel intimidated. So what if he thinks he is a March / Ivory Coast / R and looks like Peter Pan. I am an August / Colombia / B and look like Pocahontas. I even worked out a model to finance the networking app. Advertising by therapists. They wouldn't know your name but could have pay for targeted adverts that say things like "Relating to Belgium is often a sign of split personality, would either of you like to talk to someone about that?" or "Do you secretly feel you are a Q, call us for help to change". Anyone with a Peter Pan would automatically get a "Commitment issues? We can help you become an adult".

It was no different at the park. I stood at the entrance quietly so as not to disturb anyone. My eyes saw a peaceful bench in the corner under a tree. It was a good bench, just far enough back from the main path that people walking by would not have to avoid my feet, and I could avoid their gaze. Open enough that people could see it was already occupied so not approach in hope of finding a place to sit. The view of other people was good. Would be assassins, Jehovah's witnesses, and other dangers could be detected in advance and plans made to foil their approach before they got too close. All this was good, but it had ignored one parameter. Canines. As I walked with purpose towards the bench, but not so much purpose that I could not change direction without embarrassment if someone got to it before me, so I gained a 'friend'. I am not sure what sort of canine he was, but he was loud. I have heard there is a breed of canine called Singing Dogs that come from New Guinea. My new friend was to them as a baby screaming is to Mozart. Pushing a pram with a crying baby would have been softer on my ears and less conspicuous to others enjoying this green and verdant space. The dog was not angry with me, in fact he seemed pleased to see me. I suspected he had mistakenly recognised me as some old friend who many years ago gave him the best tummy tickle of his life. Like some narcoleptic dog he ran around me and every so often suddenly fell over on his back to show me his belly. When no hand reached down to stroke it, he would bolt back up as if an elec-tro cardio shock had brought him back to life, and the barking would restart. I could see some people looking at me and clearly asking why this man could not control his noisy dog. There is no symbol for 'this is not my dog'. I waved my hand to indicate my displeasure and make clear it was not mine, but hoping it was not look so disgruntled that people would think I was not a dog lover. Being seen as a dog hater in a park is much like the man who mis-takenly bring pork sausages to a vegan BBQ. In my defence no one told me, and who really believes there is such a thing as a vegan BBQ? It is clearly an oxymoron.

I arrived at the bench and sat down. A hotel room would have been better because you have a door to close. With no walls or door to protect me I remained a victim of loving canine attention. He sat to attention. A meter in front of me and looking intently for any sign in my slightly rigid body that I might want to play with him. I looked away to my left. His head swivelled to match my gaze. I looked to my right and he followed my gaze. It was like looking in a mirror that showed my inner dog reflection. As my head went up so he raised his. I tried making a circular motion, and he followed. It was a little bit freaky. A fly buzzed in-front of my eyes and I raised a hand to flick it away. My companion raised a paw past his nose.

I got a book out and started to read it while ensuring it was at the right height to stop any direct eye contact between either of us. In the corner of my eye I saw a lady with a small Pekinese approaching along the path. I felt more confident. Everybody knows that a Pekinese dog will bark at anything, especially another dog. Even better it was on a lead. For some reason being on a lead always makes a dog more likely to bark. They know that being on a lead is a sign their owner wants protecting. I was right. As she approached a yapping started up. The pesky Pekinese was clearly telling my new companion to back off. I waited for the response. Barks saying the equivalent of 'bring it on', 'you talking to me', 'your owner looks like a cat'. There was nothing. I lowered my book to check he was still there. He was. In fact, he had stretched out on the grass and had that foolish happy look all dogs get. The lady with the Pekinese stopped. The yapping continued from her feet. The silence continued from mine. "What a nice dog you have" she said. For some reason I nodded. She smiled and carried on down the path while her Pekinese found a new threat to her life that it would protect her from. It looked at a lost glove on the path. Probably a roadside bomb it thought and barked once more. It might have been a gust of wind, but to me it looked as if the lost glove raised a single middle finger to the dog.

I put down my book and started to think. I looked around. There was a small branch on the ground by the bench. I reached down for it. The dog opened one eye. I started to show a deep interest in the stick. "what a great stick", "must be oak". The dog sat up. I caressed the stick. It was the most desirable stick in the world. I looked at him "do you want it?" "you want this stick?". He was listening to my every word and watching my every movement. He knew something was coming. I waved the stick towards him and away, then with a mighty movement threw it over his head. He watched it sail through the air and land in the distant grass. Then he looked at me to see what I would do. I looked at him and then at the stick, then back to him. Nothing. "Go get the stick". Nothing. There was a sudden sound of running. A stick appeared at my feet. The same stick I had just thrown. Beside it was a black Labrador who looked into my eyes, then stared down at the stick, then back to my eyes. My companion looked at the Labrador, looked at the stick, looked at me, then lay down once more.

I reasoned both these dogs must have owners. Irresponsible owners, but owners. I scanned the park. There were various potential owners. People on benches, people walking without a dog, even families picnicking. I was used to this irresponsible behaviour. On occasion young children had done something similar to me. They would approach, stare and even ask questions like "are you the nasty man my mother told me about?". At first, I tried saying "yes" to scare them off. This would work for about five minutes before a policeman would approach me and ask me to leave the park. I tried saying "no" but that just resulted in further questions. My current approach was to ignore them or pretend to be Bolivian. I stood up. The two dogs jumped to attention. I would walk round the park. As I set off my two companions started to follow me. First the Labrador, still carrying the stick, followed by my original companion. Now there were three of us it was a much more sedate affair. More of a procession. I clearly was their alpha male and they would follow me wherever I felt the pack needed to go. I approached a small girl standing by the path sucking some liquid up through a straw from a carton. As we approached, she removed the straw. "I like your dogs". "They are not my dogs". "Then why are you taking them for a walk". "I am not. They are following me". She put the straw back in her mouth and took a large suck on it while digesting this information. I carried on. I heard a sucking sound from behind me. The girl had joined our procession. I gave her a hard look. She gave me back a hard look. I carried on.

I started to weave a slightly erratic course. Like a child drawing by joining the dots so a ensured my walk went past any potential dog owners. We got admiring looks, but no recognition. I nearly completed a full circuit and arrived back at the park gate I had entered by. I pondered whether I could run fast enough out of the gate to lose them all. I figured I could outrun the little girl. The Labrador looked a little fat so he might be beatable. My original friend looked far too fit. Then brilliance struck. I slowly walked to the entrance gate. The procession was a few steps behind me. I made a sudden lunge and pulled the gate of the park closed making a barrier between me and my companions. The little girl stood and eyed me thoughtfully, her lips pursed either in deep thought or to get extra suction on her straw. The black Labrador just carried on walking forward. The tip of his nose could protrude between the bars to my side, but he had not allowed for the branch in his mouth. He seemed to treat it like one of those infernal metal puzzles you get at Christmas. He tried his nose through another part of the gate, then another. He started to look some sort of robotic vacuum cleaner just hitting itself against the gate waiting for some instruction to change direction. The smaller dog, like the girl, just stared at me, clearly bright enough to understand when he was beaten by a superior mind. After all no dog had invented fire or the wheel. It crossed my mind that maybe dogs had just let man invent fire, then once invented let man collect the wood necessary before the dog turned up and stretched out by the fire. If true, then I and all mankind were in trouble. I looked at my two ex-canine companions and I knew Darwin was right, Evolution was a competitive race and Christians were right since it was clear that man was the winner.

There was an extra bounce to my step as I left the park to the shade of four-story town houses casting their darkness across pavements. While I would not boast out loud about beating two dogs and a small girl, however it was an affirmation of my standing and superior intellect, I was thinking it to myself. As American football coaches endlessly make clear, you can either be a winner or a looser, and I was a winner.

Outside of the park the pace of life picked up. People kept passing me who clearly had somewhere to be. Some coming towards me like a bullet to be dodged. Others coming up behind me, announced by their rapid footstep. Some were on their phones explaining, for reasons I have never understood, what they were doing and where they were. "I'm walking on Turnball Road". Were the people at the other end saying things like "I'm in the kitchen at 7 Acacia Avenue" or "I'm on a train to Crew and we just passed a field with a cow in". People on trains always like to tell other people they are on a train. The only impulse stronger is when people land after a flight and call other people to tell them they have landed. My phone, possibly feeling left out, made a short twinkling noise. Like a security officer at Heathrow airport I started patting my body down to find which pocket I had left my phone in. As I removed it a bronze coin fell out of the pocket onto the pavement and rolled away. A wandering pigeon out for a stroll stared for one moment at the image of her majesty on the coin. His head went to one side as his rather small mind tried to process what he was seeing. Like many creatures it resorted to the default decision of 'peck and see if its edible'. It wasn't so he moved on. When I was younger a story used to be told that if Bill Gates, at that time the richest man in the world, was walking down a street and came across a one hundred dollar note on the ground, it would not be financially cost effective for his time to bend over and pick it up. While not as rich as Mr Gates, I felt that a two pence piece was probably at the limit of where I valued my time, so I carried on walking. The message on my phone screen said, 'get rolls, sausages and wine'. It seemed the sunshine had brought out the BBQ for our evening supper. On other occasions a message such as this might have caused me to sigh and mutter about people who cannot plan properly. However today the sunshine and my triumph escaping the park told me I was a man for whom words like 'spontaneous' and 'carefree' were a moral code to live by. I relished the prospect of walking down our high street in search of locally produced product from artisan farmers.

High street may be too grand a word even though a man on a mobile phone passed me saying 'I am walking down the High Street'. It was officially called the High Street. I am sure in its day it was the height of sophisticated shopping, where local gentry of breeding, and hence of high class, did their shopping. I assume that's why all these places are called High Street – the street that high-class people frequent. It was inconceivable that it was named after the fact the short people were banned from walking along it. Or might it have been one of those names that has changed spelling subtly. Were they originally the place where unemployed labourers looking for work loitered in hope of a 'gig' picking hops or fruit in local fields? The Hired Street. I have no idea, but I entered number 14 the High Street in search of rolls. Many years ago, it had just been a bakery. You could buy iced buns and Eccles cakes. Today it proclaimed itself an Artisan Baker. Many things in the high street seemed to be artisan. That or charity shops. As for the derivation of the word artisan - I always quite liked the idea that it was really part of a sentence starting 'Art is an..' in reference to someone called Arthur and his profession. Art is an apple seller. Art is an umbrella maker. Art is an embalmer. My bonhomie to mankind was growing. "Good-day" I announced as I grandly entered. This was created by a "Hello luv". I suspected the artisan was out creating and her sister, the part time child minder, was minding the shop. "I have come in search of your best rolls". There was a pause, a slight look of embarrassment as my newfound friend looked at the shelves. "I'm sorry we are out of rolls". A wave of disappointment crossed my face. Seeing my despair, she looked round for salvation "We do have buns". I frowned "Aren't buns cakes for elephants?". "We have sweet buns, but also savoury buns... I am not sure of the exact difference between a roll and a savoury bun". "probably the price" I said with a smile and good humour. Her honesty shone through "Oh no, everything's expensive here so they are a similar price to our rolls". This seemed promising "What the choice of savoury bun?". Traditionally I was used to choices like white, brown or seeded. Of course, no artisan baker would be able to justify their prices with descriptions like that. "We have saffron with basil made with linseed; these are pumpkin with Spanish sundried tomato and Sicilian black olives; and these are chicory infused gluten free flour with " and she paused and looked at me "your not a police officer are you?". I am by nature honest so admitted I was not. She continued in a hushed voice "... with marijuana". Now I understood what artisan meant. It also gave a new possible meaning to High Street. I ordered six of the saffron with basil. You may think of me as a prude for not going with the marijuana, but they were gluten free and it just seemed too great a contradiction. Anything 'something' free should never be combined with pleasure seeking. If anything, they should have been making marijuana buns with extra gluten. The lady placed them in a brown bag that had swirly writing on the side to inform me it was biodegradable and made by lepers in Nepal. She tied a purple hemp string bow round the top of it to seal it. I couldn't bring myself to then put it in my reusable plastic Tesco shopping bag which still had Christmas written all over it. I went in search of sausages.

I entered the butcher, who the sign informed was also a licensed handler of game. Inside was like an episode of The Sopranos done by David Attenborough. There was a deer hanging upside down in one corner. It must have committed some terrible crime, probably to a Mexican cartel, since it was missing its head. On the walls next to it were rows of hooks with various species of duck that had not paid back some loan and been turned into examples in case other ducks came passing by. The glass counter had displays of meat on skewers, meats sewn up into parcels, meat pies with different layers like geological ages you could bite through, and sausages of different sizes, shades and shapes. A woman in a smart fake fur coat was eyeing up different joints so I jumped ahead of her and presented myself for business. The man in the white blood-stained apron inspected me. As his eyes passed over the parcel from the artisan bakery, he started to move slightly to the left of the counter, which was the end containing steak, wild boar, and pre made beef wellingtons. I had been appraised, and the conclusion was I had money to spend, a man truly worthy of shopping in the high street. I looked him in the eye and said one word "Sausages". He looked back at me "Sorry sir we don't allow dogs in the shop". I looked at him, he looked at me. For a split second I looked at the woman next to me. "Dog?". His eyes just looked down to my left, then back up at me. I turned and looked down. My friend from the park had appeared like some canine genie. "That's not my dog". "He came in with you and is sitting next to you". "True but the fact remains he is not my dog". "Whose dog is he?". "I don't know". "Why is he looking at you like he knows you?". "We met earlier in the park". "So, you do know the dog". "Well as well as I know you". "Then could you ask him to leave the shop please". I was slightly flummoxed by this request. "How would you suggest I do that?". "Well just ask him. You know him as well as you know me, and you could ask me so why can't you ask him?". Clearly, I had offended this man in his blood-soaked apron, who spent his day chopping, hacking and filleting dead bodies. I guess butchers have feelings, you just don't expect it when as a culture people have nicknames like 'the butcher of berlin' or 'the butcher of Leningrad'. "Sorry, it was not my intention to suggest my friendship with you and with this dog were similar. Rather I wanted to make clear this dog was not a close acquaintance who I can persuade to do things, and even if he was... he is a dog!". It could have gone either way at this point. I mean we might have had to have the BBQ without artisan sausages.

However true British spirit won the day and a got a smile of understanding from across the counter. Not only did this break any ice that may have formed between us, but it also gave me the momentum to take the initiative. I turned to fully face the dog, raised my arm to point to the door and in a commanding voice instructed the dog to leave the building. He clearly understood this was a communication. His ears were raised, his head tilted, and his eyes were intently looking at mine. Had he been human he would be a great date. You could see him thinking 'what does that mean?'. As a species they may not be as sophisticated and erudite, but there was no doubt this was a thinking dog. He got to all fours, then flipped himself over onto his back and presented his stomach to me expectantly. I upped my game. My most angry shout and haughtiest look. He wagged his tail faster.

I looked at the butcher who now understood this was not my dog. No words were exchanged but he came around from behind his counter to join me. We both understood an alliance had been formed. He tried his best words "Shoo!", "Scram!", "Be off with you!". The tail just wagged more frantically. I was thinking it, and I suspected he was too. We needed physical force. However, this was England. It was perfectly acceptable to kill and eat a lamb, but violence against a dog would ensure attacks on social media - anti-social media in fact - as well as letters to the local paper about the cruelty of the local butcher who uses force to remove a dog from his shop. I had an idea that could give plausible denial. "Do you have a broom?" I asked. I guess all butchers are men of action, this one certainly was. No further words were necessary. He made Clint Eastwood in a western look chatty. Two steps behind the counter, and then two steps back with a broom in his out-stretched hand. I took the broom and looked around. "Do you have any security cameras in here?". He shook his head. I extended the broom to-wards the dog. As the bristles touched his stomach so his tongue came out in what I took to be an ex-pression of delirious pleasure. Clearly his hopes and wishes had come true and the bristles were tickling his stomach. In his mind he had understood the human instructions, taken the appropriate action, and was now being rewarded with the sweet pleas-ure of a belly rub. In my mind he was a pest. I pushed slightly harder and he just lay back in pleasure like some roman emperor with his concubines adoring him. The lady next to me had turned to watch. "How sweet". I suspected she might be a potential letter writer to the editor of the local paper, so I had to be careful. I upped the pressure a little more. Physics was not my strongest subject at school, but some line about equal and opposite forces came to my mind. Then suddenly they were equal no more. His glossy fur sitting on the tiled floor had a low threshold of friction to overcome. Like a ship being launched, his body began to slide along the floor as I brushed him towards the door. If you have ever watched the sport of curling on the winter Olympics you will have the perfect picture. It is possible that the first games of curling were in fact Eskimos pushing sleeping huskies out of their igloos by sliding them across the ice with a whale bone handle broom. My smooth pressure was now building up power. I stopped. He kept on sliding. Still on his back, still with his tail wagging. He slid past the counter, past the cardboard cut-out of a pig with the words 'Eat Me' embossed on it, and out the shop door into the High Street. The sound of a series of braking cars indicated I may have applied too much pressure. I dared not look for fear of seeing a body in the road under a car. My only consolation was that if he was dead, we had a butcher on hand to rapidly remove any evidence of my heinous crime. There was a sharp intake of breath from the lady next to me.

A wave of relief came over me as his head reappeared through the door with his unharmed body following behind. In fact, he came running in at speed. Stopped at the foot of the broom and rolled over once more on to his back. "Oh it's a game" exclaimed the lady who was once more smiling. The butcher and I smiled back. Much as a priest smiles back at a child in Sunday school who asks, "do angels go to the toilet?". The dog gave a little yap to encourage us to repeat the game. "Would you like a go?" I asked as I proffered the broom to the lady. "Could I?" but it was rhetorical, she took the broom. "Half a dozen sausages please" I quickly said to the butcher. He understood time was short and hurried back round to his side of the counter. The lady was using the brush more like a feather duster that was tickling the ecstatic dog. A parcel of sausages was passed across the counter. She lined the brush up with her new friend and started to push him across the floor as I was passing a ten-pound note across the counter. "weeee" she cried as he went sliding out the door. Again, the sound of cars braking could be heard. We all stopped moving and looked at the door. No nose appeared. There was more car sounds outside. The lady's face started to elongate as if Edward Munch had decided to paint her. "Oh my god" she exhaled. Like some parent who had been throwing their child in the air to only miss the catch as they fell back to earth. She started for the door and I turned to the butcher "Do you have a back door?". Like some British airman escaping the gestapo he led me through a curtain to a door at the back. I nodded, shook his hand, turned and ran.

On arriving at the off licence, the door was blocked by a man looking out at a distant crowd further down the high street. I nodded to indicate my wish to enter and he moved to one side. "Sorry, just looking to see what the commotion is down the high street. Any idea what's happening?". I turned and pretended it was the first I had seen of it. The gods above certainly had a dark sense of humour. In the distance I could make out two vans parked side by side. The first said 'Pet Ambulance', the second 'Butcher - we supply all sorts of meat'. I turned back to the doorman "No idea" and walked in heading briskly to the shelves marked 'Sale'. The doorman had moved over with me and now becoming the salesman. His goal being to migrate me from the 'Sale' shelves to the 'Premium' section.

"Is it for a special occasion?" he enquired. Like I would fall for that. Well I did once when I admitted it was for an anniversary. On that occasion the trap shut within seconds "Then you may want to consider something suitable for such an important event". There is no way you can be seen to buy from the Sale shelf once you have admitted it needs to be special. "No, it is just something for the emergency wine shelf" I replied coolly and in a way that made clear I would only be drinking this when all the other bottles of wine in my house had run out, and with the clear message this was a low value purchase. I was feeling aggressive and decided to lead with psychology. "What's your cheapest bottle?". A pained look crossed his face. "We have nothing cheap in stock... but this would be our lowest priced bottle" he said pointing to the very bottom corner of the Sale section. I reached down and brought the dusty bottle out of the shade into semi sunlight to inspect its label. "Mongolian Pink Nun... I am not sure I know it". "Its very niche, we find it mainly brought by pet owners celebrating their pet's birthday, many bring it back to us suggesting it made their pet sick". He was upping his game and had succeeded in moving up one rung on the pricing ladder, but I was still feeling combative. "What is your lowest price wine that does not make pets sick?". It was as if I had rung the bell for the second round, he was ahead but a knockout blow like that should have finished the fight in my favour. It didn't. "This wine is popular with students and other people new to wine" he said as he passed me a bottle from the middle of the Sale shelf. "I'm told it suits the palette of 17-year-old girls, if you entertain such crowds?". His smugness was hidden but like an assassin in the darkness I could see its outline as a shadow across his face". I looked at the bottle. Turned it over in my hand and ran my finger along the writing to show I was considering it. Of course, I could not take it now he had implied it was good for paedophiles with no knowledge of wine. I fought back "Do you do a bulk discount for this wine?". "I'm sorry Sir, nothing in the sale section has a bulk discount, may I suggest we look at this section for wines where we offer 'six bottles for the price of five'". We moved sideways away from the Sale to the next area of shelves entitles "Great Value". He had won the second round. I needed a new tactic to wear him down. "Do you have any white wines from Madagascar?". "I am not aware that Madagascar make white wine sir, were you perhaps thinking of Moldova?". "No, it's Madagascar, I saw a review of them in the Sunday paper food magazine. It said I should be able to find some at all good wine stores". I placed a lot of emphasis on the word 'good'. Third round to me I thought. I was wrong again. "We tend not to stock populist wines based on reviews in colour supplements. Our selection process is more about experience and palate. Take this wine" he reached to shelf on the next section across "it was awarded the Medallion d'Obtuse this year by the international wine tasters association". I decided to call round three a draw. I don't know what happened at that point. Maybe I could feel I was losing. I panicked. "I don't like the picture on the label". As soon as I said it, I knew I was in trouble. I knew he knew I was in trouble. I knew he knew that I knew I was in trouble. "What sort of labels does sir normally like to select his wine by?" He emphasised 'labels' the same was I had emphasised 'good' earlier. Revenge was sweet. "Well it's not me, rather it's my wife who has a thing about funny labels". It was both a desperate sad tactic but a good tactic. He couldn't argue with a wife that wasn't in the shop. "She's a lady of taste?". I felt guilty for slurring her good name, so I admitted she was a lady of taste. On hearing this he moved across to the 'Premium' section "This is where ladies of taste normally select from" and his arm waved across the shelves inviting me to inspect the quality much as a jeweller does on hearing a husband is looking for a diamond necklace that says 'Sorry' to appease an irate wife. "Which is your best value Premium Wine?" I heard myself saying. "Could I recommend this one. It is not the lowest in price, but it has an exquisite aroma the reminds one of summer pastures. It goes very well with fish and seafood". "Were having a sausage BBQ". He looked pained. "Free range organic sausages sourced locally of course" I added quickly. He smiled recognising we had reached an implicit limit to his work "This also goes very well with artisan sausages sir. How many bottles would you like?"

Have you seen all these bicycles you can rent for an hour using your mobile phone? Well I want to know why they don't do the same thing with donkeys or camels. When you have six bottles of expensive wine, a bag of organic ethically assassinated sausages, and artisan rolls, a bicycle is not enough. Even today you don't see traders travelling through Himalayan passes or crossing the sand dunes of the Sahara carrying goods on a bicycle. The only person I can think of who uses a bicycle for carrying goods is the French man in Bretton top and beret, with rolls of garlic strung around his body while cycling along in search of English customers. Even this may be a myth since like dragons I have only seen such creatures in pictures and Disney movies. The 'free' sixth bottle of wine was starting to annoy me. It was a bit like buying five feathers and being given and extra golden feather for free, which sounds good but actually more than doubles the weight you need to carry. Somehow the free sixth bottle seemed heavier than the rest and it kept causing the cardboard box to tilt with its weight. I struggled on, the box of wine under one arm, the edible items clutched by the hand at the end of the other arm.

Do you believe there is such a thing as an unforgivable crime? Well if you do then by implication there must be forgivable crimes. Would a devout puritan consider it acceptable to commit a small indiscretion if it helped others? My line between good and evil is somewhere higher than the puritans', so I positively rejoiced to find an abandoned shopping trolley stuck in a bush at the side of the path. Like many shopping trolleys I have little idea how it got here miles from any parking lot where its brethren formed orderly lines waiting to be pushed and pulled along the aisles of merchandise. I saw a documentary once that explained how new species of plant arrived on remote pacific islands carried stuck to birds' feet. I wondered if something similar happened but with people who find their jumper stuck to the trolley in some way and are only able to shake it off after some distance from the supermarket. Did some abandoned shopping trolleys take root in the ground and gradually turn into mini supermarket, before maturing many years later into a large supermarket in their own right that their parents would have been proud of.

This trolley was more like a tortoise that had fallen on its back and was unable to right itself. Four small wheels poked up into the air. A Robin was sitting on one of them looking at me. I was no longer in a mood for admiring nature. A wild wave of my hand demonstrated my supreme power to the Robin who flew off as human Godzilla approached. Putting my boxes and bags down, I turned and grabbed the trolley. Nature did not want to give it to me. Green ropes of grass and bramble held on to it like a mother afraid of losing her child. I pulled harder. The bushes around started to tremble from the violent waves that were ebbing out from our conflict. There was only one of me, and so man plants. However, the combined brain power of the plants was nowhere as great as mine. In a cunning twist I suddenly pushed the trolley away catching the green army off guard. The trolley broke free of some of them. I employed the washing powder approach. Wash and repeat. I repeatedly pulled then pushed. Each change of direction gained me a little more control of the trolley until a final pull broke it free. A broken army of grass and vines lay ravaged. To the victor his spoils.

As spoils go, a rusty discarded shopping trolley is not really up there with 'the sacking of Rome', or 'the plunder of Constantinople', however I felt good. I loaded my shopping into the trolley and pushed off for foreign lands. Shopping trolleys are of course famous for what scientists call 'emergent intelligence'. This is the concept that you can take a group of separate items, say a thousand small birds, combine them together into a flock to create life. The super organism behaves in new and seemingly intelligent ways. With the flock of birds, it's an ability to move as one, round objects, creating pulsating shapes, yet all the time without a single bird bumping into any of its nine hundred and ninety-nine neighbours flying next to it. Passengers on the London underground show some similar patterns but much simpler and with some bumping into each other. This may be called 'emergent stupidity'? A shopping trolley shows 'emergent stubbornness'. A collection of quite reasonable components, metal rods, handles, coaster wheels, are combined to create the trolley. Like magic they no longer behave as they once did. Wheels decide they don't want to go in certain directions. In turn they make handles pull you to one side and the steerer becomes the steered. The rods develop an elastic ability to flex and throw any item resting on them up short distances into the air. I would make an observation that shopping trolleys only became widespread after people ceased to bear arms. Why? Because any sane person would have shot their misbehaving trolley out of extreme irritation ten minutes after having been paired up with it. Had you plotted my route with the trolley you might have called it 'the drunkards walk'. We veered left and right, two steps back, one sideways for every one forward. My estimate was that we had travelled four hundred meters, or fifty-seven if plotted as the distance between my start and end, before I mentally shot the trolley. I removed my shopping and kicked the trolley into the bushes at the side of the path. The grasses and brambles gratefully accepted their new metal skeleton and started planning to build a new world around it.

I was getting closer to home. Goldfinch Lane is delightfully named, and full of detached houses. I don't think there are any more, or any less, goldfinches flying round it than neighbouring Caps Lane and Church Road. Some of the gardens have bird feeders, so I expect there must be some goldfinches. Its name is more honest than neighbouring Mandela Gardens, which I assume the great man never visited, unless of course his Uncle Horatio or some such distant relative had retired there. As well as bags of peanuts for the birds these gardens have flower borders, garden ornaments of various taste, and a variety of water features. You can tell they are homes to people with too much time on their hands because the hosepipes are neatly coiled, the grass is short and green. Reflecting both the age we are in, as well as British optimism, many of the water features have a solar panel nestled nearby to power the water feature. In olden times people had barometers to measure air pressure and tell them if the weather would be fair or foul. Now you can just open a window and listen for the intensity of the water feature. If you hear gushing water, then slap on the sun cream and take your tea outside.

There is a problem with this paradise. The reason the hosepipes are coiled, and the grass is short, is the same reason I had to run the gauntlet to get home. Retired men. I don't object to retired men in principle, I have friends who are retired men, I even hope to be one myself at some point in my distant future. But... and there has to be a 'but', just a red rag is said to set off a bull into a wild frenzy, so seeing someone not coping well with a practical problem makes something inside a retired man want to comment on the obvious. My staggering with food and drink was just the invitation they needed. 'Youve got a lot on your hands there' said a green cardigan inspecting his garden. 'Coping ok?' from a man still in slippers. Having provided an object of conversation for them, they started to discuss between themselves. 'I'm not sure he will make it', 'those wine bottles don't look safe', 'I hope there won't be broken glass to clear up', 'especially not if it rains' and they all look up to the sky.

A man with white hair and carrying a morning paper is coming along the pavement towards me. He doesn't move to one side. We meet, or should I say he blocks my way. I stop with an expression aiming to convey ' this is exhausting, please move out of my way'. He clearly reads it as an invitation to chat 'Youve got a heavy load there'. 'Yes' keeping it short to kill the conversation. 'Looks like you've got sausages from Huxton the butcher' more of a statement than a question but I give it a 'Yes'. 'Pork and mustard?'. I stare at him for a second 'No'. 'Chorizo?'. We couldn't go through their entire range, so I tried to cut this avenue of conversation down 'Pork and Apple'. 'Good choice ... Would you like some help?'. Annoying but sympathetic. I soften my heart a little while stiffening my arms from the weight of the wine. 'Very kind but no thank you'. 'I've got my trailer I use for the rubbish dump. I could hook it up and give you a lift?'. I recognised this trap from past experience. On retirement husbands are encouraged to put their free time to good use by their more intelligent wives. Encouragement is made to clear the house of the rubbish they have accumulated over 40 working years. The husbands push back since they have planes to build model planes. Their wives, understanding their husbands so much more than the husbands understand their wives, suggest they may want to buy a trailer to help move the rubbish. Every man wants a trailer. Men have trailers, women don't. Women have men with trailers or know men with trailers or just get stuff taken away. Excited with his new trailer the house is emptied. Even better the new trailer lives outside, so does not clutter up the now spacious house. The only problem is the man has nothing else to take in his trailer, so the search begins. Offers to help neighbours, take part in village events, help the scouts, anything if he can use his trailer. In a great twist of revenge, I once heard of a newly widowed man who to save money took his deceased wife in her coffin to the cemetery, using his trailer.

'Very kind but I only live around the corner, could I get past please, the bottles are rather heavy'. He graciously moved to one side. I set off again like a sick Sherpa determined to ascend Everest one last time. 'If you change your mind just call...'. You can't wave when carrying wine, sausages and rolls so I sort of moved my head in acknowledgement. A few more staggering paces took me around the corner beyond the sight of the cardigans and slippers. The gardens here were a little more unkempt. Some had toys scattered across their lawns. I could see my home. There was no flag flying above it, but an estate agent's sign poked out of the front proclaiming a school fete in two weeks' time. This was my north star to guide myself by. There were no neighbours in sight, no dogs wanting to play, no roadworks to go around. It was a straight flight path home. My father often would say 'don't worry about the little things in life'. This wisdom was normally shared when he was sitting in the garden with a cold drink and my mother was making lunch inside. Like most advice I have received over the years it is actually irrelevant to anything real. At this very moment it was not even correct. When a wasp lands on your nose you very much worry about the little things in life. And a wasp had landed on my nose!

You might wonder why something so small is not petrified by having two enormous, and ironically petrified, eyes staring at it up close. So close that I could just see the shape as a blur. The wasp kept turning, performing circles on my nose. Its little feet tickled. Its wings gently whirred, but not enough to take off. When you have no free arms or hands you need other ways to shoo it away. I started to move my neck side to side. Up and down. Forward and backwards. If I could do it fast enough it should fall off. It didn't. I tried sticking my lower lip out, pulling in the upper lip, and blowing hard. Nothing. My luggage was getting heavier and I had to keep moving. By now I was dancing down the street. Legs jerking from the weight I was carrying, head moving in time to invisible music to throw the wasp off. Salvation was a large alder tree at the entrance to a neighbour's drive. I repeatedly thrust my head into the branches and leaves. That did the job. The wasp flew off. I paused to regain my composure and see my neighbour with a curious expression looking out the window at me. Straightening my back, moving my chin up, I walked determinedly forward.

There is a peace to walking up the path to one's own front door. You know it's a landscape you control. Anyone who might accost you does not require polite conversation. Animals that threat you can be chastised and have things thrown at them. You are master. This is your sanctuary. After carefully placing the wine by the front door my arms felt so light and carefree. It was possible I had helium pumping through my arteries and veins. As I reached into my jacket for the house keys, my hand kept drifting upwards. It looked a bit like I was strumming a guitar as I had to keep reminding it that gravity was a universal force. The key turned in the lock. I pushed the door open. There is a second or two where you wait. Just as one pauses to smell food before eating it, so I pause to listen to the house before taking my first step inside. Is it noisy or quiet? Does an aroma of supper hit my nostrils? Can I get through the hall without negotiating an assault course of old clothing for the charity shop? The hall was clear, I was carrying supper with me, and all was quiet. I hauled up the wine box, stepped over the threshold and made one last sprint to the kitchen.

THE CAT WOMAN

The whole town runs down to the sea from the hills. Each roof top is a little lower than the previous one, creating a staircase for the cat woman. From above stars light your way. From below you are touched by shafts of light, laughter and snatches of music. Different tunes fill the air as you breathe in the night and look round. You drop your glowing cigarette to the red roof tile floor. As you gently rub its embers our with your high heel boot, you realise a real cat is sitting by a chimney, watching you. To humour him you claw your hands in the air and make a meow sound; just as you will do later when I am kissing your neck. Your journey takes you over more roof tops. The smell of barbecuing mackerel comes up from a chimney you pass. You pause to admire a man having a shower, unaware that cat women on rooftops can see his every move. In the windows next to him is a woman, his wife or lover getting changed for bed, looking at her face in the mirror. The roof tops end and you are looking out across the Atlantic

Ocean. White horses from the waves show up as the moonlight bounces off them. A dozen ships have parked a mile out to sea, creating a village of twinkling lights floating on black velvet. Just as Columbus set out on his mission from here, so do you, by swinging down onto a fire escape that leads to the streets below. On your journey down each window you pass tells a different story. The lonely 92-year-old man, remembering his childhood. The sleeping baby, awaiting her childhood. A couple watching television, another dancing slowly to the radio. In one window a ten-year-old girl is looking at the moon. She gasps when she sees you, but your quick smile and whisking of your tail at her makes her laugh, so you carry on undetected.

The streets are cobbled, the same cobbles that two hundred years ago explorers and adventurers walked on. Your shoes make a light tap as they hit each stone. The street lights create pools of yellow surrounded by black darkness, a leopard's skin pattern stretched between the buildings. You walk along the dark lines, arriving at a tall house. It has no number, no name but you already know it and what it hides inside. A glance either way shows you are still invisible to the world. You run, then jump, grabbing hold of a first-floor balcony. Years of yoga make it easy to pull your way up on to it. Breathing a little faster now, straining then relaxing your cream breasts against the tight black suit, you create pulsating flashes in the moonlight. Another jump and climb take you to the top floor. Now surrounded by iron railing and pots of plants releasing a musky perfume into the night air. Reaching to your left boot you make a gesture. A blade has appeared. You slide it round the window frame, the same way you cut a joint of chicken, pause, then push the window up and open. You dive in, head first.

It's a bedroom with a large velvet bed in the middle. Modern paintings grace the walls. You study each one carefully. One you recognise. With confidence you move to the painting of a wolf guarding a lost baby in a forest. Pulling at a corner of the painting reveals a cupboard in the wall. It also shows it has an over confident owner. Inside is a single necklace. You take it. Turning around you unzip a pocket in your tail and drop the necklace into its new home. Like an oyster closing to hide the pearl, you zip the tail back up. Looking round you take a pen and paper from a nearby table. With slow gestures of grace, you write "meow" then kiss the paper leaving a lipstick smudge. Dropping it in the cupboard, you put the picture back and head to the window. The adrenalin has made you hungry for food and ravenous for passion. Two street down is the sound of laughter and music. You turn the corner to see a square full of coloured lights strung out between the trees. Footsteps behind you are coming up fast. As you turn you see a police-man heading your way. He is looking straight at you. "Nice costume" he says and walks on. In the square people are dancing, but not any people. There is a fireman, a pirate, a nurse, a princess, and every other profession or char-acter imaginable. You follow the policeman and start looking for something, or someone, to eat. A hand grabs your waist from behind and spins you round. Batman is looking into your eyes, he pauses and runs his other hand down your tight cat suit, then looking you straight in the eye, bends forward slowly, and kisses you. "where the hell have you been?" he asks. You kiss him again, then pushing his head back and meeting his gaze say, "it's a long tail".

OSLO PARK

From above the park had become a piebald pony. Pools of dark shade from the trees splashed across a sea of glaring reflection from the burnt-out grass waiting for rain. Individual sunbathers were sprinkled like hundreds and thousands with their pink, yellow and blue blankets to stretch out on. The couples stayed in the shadows of the trees. Intimate conversations by intimate people. Still unsure of their relationships and not wanting to place themselves under the full glare of the sun for inspection by people walking their dogs or pushing their prams. The heat was a contradiction, evaporating away any moisture to create dry crumbly soil, yet generating sweat on every sunbather and walker to moisten what little clothing they were wearing to stay respectable. At the top of the hill there were no trees, so no shade. It gave a great view of the city, and occasionally, when the gods were generous, it gave a light breeze. Whenever the breeze could be felt arms and legs would open a little wider to let it in, like water lilies opening and closing in response to sunshine and clouds passing over. The peak had a plateau. Probably man made, since when does nature prefer a line to a curve? In the middle was a jade rectangle of shallow water with low concrete sides. Whatever its creator had intended it for, it was now a paddling pool dominated by dog walkers and their charges. The smallest dogs had to swim like wind-up toys crossing a very large bath. The rest could stand. Some up to their shoulder, some to their belly, and a few just to their knees. The swimming dogs never put their heads below the water, but rather changed direction with random purpose on seeing other dogs they liked or feared. Canine bumper cars moving with magnets built in to repel and attract. Their human owners rose up like cypress trees in a swamp. Their roots embedded bellow the water which hid their wiggling toes. Women held raised skirts with one hand, while shielding their eyes, or gesticulating with the other. Little mounds at the sides of the pool marked the spots where the men with shorts had removed their sandals as if entering a mosque. The men with trousers just stood warily at the side, watching their dog and trying to decide what the right balance of pleasure for their hot charges was versus health for their own skin from the relentless burning sun. There was laughter and gentle conversation as dog owners watched their fur covered companions discover new friends, play, and sometimes fall out with each other. Unlike in winter, there was very little shouting or barking. Every species realised it was too hot for that.

Three hundred meters from the park, is another

park. To get to it you need to travel through streets of coffee shops providing recovery for exhausted runners, grocers selling pallets of ruby raspberries and second-hand booksellers hoping for rain that would drive street walkers into their shops. I say another park but officially it's a cemetery. But really it is a park. There are no sunbathers. Not just because it looks bad to sunbathe next to resting dead people, but also because the climate is so different here. Tall obelisks and dark headstones. Everyday life giving water is sprayed across the land ensuring this park stays green and cool. The trees look more relaxed. Everything is relaxed. The people sitting on the benches have no hurry in their life. The families carrying flowers in search of a relative's grave have set time aside for this. The fieldfares hopping and turning over leaves, do so with a leisurely confidence in the knowledge there is plenty of food here for everyone. More evidence that this may be paradise is the perpetual gentle breeze. It makes the leaves gently chatter and wave to each other. It takes away the need to sweat but is not so strong as to dry out anything it touches. It gives life to the individual flowers planted by the headstone but is not so strong to blow the petals off. Could it be that the head stones act like mini canyons, channelling what little movement of air there is to combine and form the breeze? The headstones are like an international army. They come in many different shades. Some are tall. Some are wide. What makes them an army is the way they all stand to attention, creating lines

of rock soldiers a body length apart, and all facing
the same direction as if waiting for an instruction to
salute. Each has a name. Some have two names. A
roll call of the spirits that have been allowed to rest
in paradise. A sudden but pleasant whooshing
sound starts up from one side. A lady is filling a
watering can with water from a hose. Once full the
peace returns, and she carries it off. Unlike the first
park which is 'used' by people, this one is tendered
by people. It receives love from its visitors who
plant, weed and water to feed both the plant life,
but also their memories and souls. The park is the
combined creation of living and dead people. Each
influencing the other. Long gone parents making
their children act with reverence. Occasionally,
someone walks through with purpose. Striding rather than ambling. They have a place and a time to
be somewhere. I imagine they hold their breath as
they enter the park. Like some underwater swim-
mer they must get to the other side without coming
up for air. If they fail and take a gulp of the cool life-
giving air, then their pace will slow with each in-
hale. Some make it through, safe in the knowledge
their life still has importance. Others fail but find
new meaning to their day. They look at the names
on the gravestones and it makes them ask what is
important. None of the headstones say, "She did a
great sales pitch" or "He was always on time". Rather
they talk about who loved them, who missed them
when they went, who still may visit their memory.
With these thoughts often comes peace rather than

urgency. For some it is too painful to think about. They double their pace once more and promise to book more meetings rather than find new friendships. For them sunbathing in the other park is safer.

Across the road from the cemetery is a different sort of cemetery. The window displays bones, dead bodies, and inorganic items of ancient origin. Some are marked 'bestseller'. What once were bodies have now become stone. The owner is a short bald man. His office is a square area of glass cabinets with a cash machine. A large dominating pillar hides him. His voice rings out a welcome, but as I search to see its source all I get is a shadow on the wall behind the pillar. A step to the left and I get a face "let me know if you have any questions". I have none and too many, all at the same time. Most of what my eyes can see means nothing to me but calls to me like toys in a toy shop. Fossils, skeletons, and bird's half brought back to life through taxidermy. Rows of small boxes containing different semi-precious stones looking like some exotic pill box from Wonderland. I am tempted by everything. Could I use a mammoth tooth dredged up from the North Sea as a paperweight on my desk? Would a small slice of jade like Amazonite be a romantic gift for my partner? I settle on a scorpion embedded in Perspex. On paying the owner compliments me on my great choice of purchase. As I leave his shop and return to the road I glance back across to the cemetery. I am carrying one dead creature entombed in Perspex. Across the road are another hundred entombed in wood and stone.

BEACH BAR

The sign says, "Beach Bar". There is a row of white cabanas laid out like children's building blocks, but with a string of fairy lights to join them together. Little straw hats on top of wooden poles form a collection of unruly middle earth characters waiting to come to life. Deck chairs face the water, ready for worship to the sun god. To hold it all together this is a rectangular wooden bar, with skyscraper stools where you can sit, and idly stir your cocktail.

The seagulls calling overhead are the only living thing occupying this Caribbean façade. People walk past it, and round it, as if a leper were sleeping in their midst. People dressed in black. Black leggings, black coats, black shoes. Who wears black to a beach bar? Who puts a beach bar in the middle of an English shopping centre?

There are no palm trees. Someone has stolen the azure blue sky that holiday brochures assure us comes with a beach bar. The water is real, but the canal boats on it are not filled with scantily clad women building their perfect tan. Only the 'humorous' captains hat worn by passing gin palace skippers joins the two worlds together. Do they also have a shopping trolley recover problem on Caribbean beaches?

If you get bored twirling that little cocktail umbrella in your drink, you can have a quick dip for a change. A dip into Debenhams for that swimsuit you forgot, a dip into Pizza Hut for that food you miss, a dip into a Vue Cinema to escape the rain.

Some young people stop and look. They chat and laugh, then descend the stairs like children going through the wardrobe to Narnia. Once inside they become more animated, touching things, standing next to things. A head with a wild mop of hair appears inside the wooden bar. Maybe he had spent the night sleeping there. He points to a blackboard. There is more laughter as the youngsters find an excuse to repeat names like 'slow comfortable screw'. Agreement is reached. Money changes hands and the visitors have become customers.

The human mop starts collecting bottles, finding sharp knives, selecting fruit and a diversity of glass shapes. The customers drift to the seating and start debating the merits of cabanas versus deck chairs. The smartphones start to appear from pockets and handbags. Poses are struck and buttons are pushed to capture the moment. The mop becomes impressively animated dissecting the fruit, crushing the ice, measuring coloured fluids from the bottles. An alchemist at work. The cabanas win the vote, after all their parents had deckchairs. Drinks arrive on a tray, paper umbrellas protecting the ice from the grey sky with its lukewarm sun. More poses are struck, glass in hand, flirting with the smartphone cameras.

Maybe that answers the question 'why build a beach bar in an English shopping centre?'. It is not for the exotic drinks they could get in any other bar. It is not because the English climate will change when you stand under a straw beach umbrella. It is because it provided the props and opportunity to post something different on your Instagram channel. To say you did something different today.

OSLO WALK
IN WOOD

It was a Sunday morning bus. Not a late morning bus that would have been full of late risers out to visit relatives or browse shops. Not an early morning bus that would have been empty or at best occupied be people on their way to bed. Just a Sunday morning bus. My getting on board had brought the total number of passengers to four, and one of them was an off-duty bus driver clearly on his way home to bed. The roads were just as empty, as were the pavements. The lady bus driver had a problem with the lack of passengers not getting on and not getting off. She clearly kept getting ahead of her schedule. We kept stopping for a minute in front of a deserted bus stop to pass time and get back on schedule. The Oslo bus service is punctual and having buses turn up before their expected time would have been both unprofessional and unacceptable. Luckily it was also unthinkable so the question never arose as how you might complain about a bus being too early. Before each stop an automated voice would announce the name of the stop and a digital display would show the name. After three months I still had difficulty matching what I heard to what I read. Certain letters were not pronounced, and there was no clue in the letter order as to which. The beauty of the written word is that people don't drop letters randomly out of them so it's much more reliable as a way to find a place. I suddenly realised this must be what it is like for deaf people - no trying to guess what a person said based on accent and local culture, rather someone writes it down and you have a 99% chance of understanding first time what they mean. My disembarkment point came up on the display. I pushed the big red 'Stop' button which as always gave me an empowering feeling. With one push of my finger I could bring this large vehicle to a stop and make everyone wait while I got off.

The bus pulled away and I was alone. The road was no longer an artery of the city but more like a dried-up riverbed, bereft of life and movement. I crossed the tarmac and headed up the hill on a track going between residential homes. Every second garden had a raised circular child cage, made out of a bouncy rubber floor with high netting walls. It was uphill and I was out of shape. I had never really been in shape. I am a shape, just not 'the shape'. My out of shape body was accompanied by an equally out of shape shadow. There are times when my shadow is in better shape than myself. If I can get the angle of light right, and the elevation of the land it lands on suitable, then my shape can be a god like Adonis able to leap boulders and bend tree branches. When

I get it wrong, its worse than a fairground mirror. I can lose limbs. Have enlarged bellies and foreheads. The only solution is to temporarily kill my shadow head by heading to a dark corner and drowning him in the black darkness of a larger shadow. Today was a mosaic of shadows cast by scattered trees, so I stayed friends with my shadow as he kept abandoning me then returning.

The houses dropped away behind me as the trees won the battle to control the land. The tarmac stopped. The gravel track began. With every step I created a crushing noise of stones rubbing together from the pressure of my heel. Was I really that noisy? I tried to change the angle which my feet hit the ground. It made no difference. I was the elephant in the forest, except an elephant in a forest is so much quieter. Gradually my ears learned to tune out my footsteps and I started to hear the life of the forest that was drawing me in. High pitched trills from invisible birds high in the canopy like audible stars above me. White noise from the wind finding its way between the leaves. Slowing down then speeding up. With each sound I felt more alive. My senses became more acute. My eyes began to see patterns in the moss on the rocks. leaves were no longer green. Emerald, pistachio, lime, mint, avocado, shamrock, viridian. The previously flat forest floor became more textured than a hippy in thick jumper and corduroy jacket. Everything became alive. Ants moved across the floor and ascending tree trunks. Spider webs reflecting sunshine as they stretched and shrunk in the wind. Birds became shooting stars, catching my eye but never staying long enough to focus on. The Schrodinger's cat of the forest - you know where they had been but not where they were now. The trees were no longer lines of identical soldiers. They became a classroom of tall, short, fat, unkept, respectable, eager, sleepy children. Their leaves became collectable item. Not quite snowflakes but not made on a production line in a factory. Some were more transparent only gently taxing the sunlight passing through. Others with black undersides took all the sunlight they could get. Round leaves, elongated leaves. Leaves with pointy corners, leaves with serrated edges, leaves in the process on unfurling their green flag. Each leaf was a microcosm of the forest around it. Bugs, beetles, and miniature spiders were at work turning each leaf into a little planet with its own life forms.

There is an old riddle about is it that can push you over, but you cannot touch, that you can hear, but never see, that destroys worlds and creates white horses. The wind. For me the wind has always been a person. Sometimes male, sometimes female. She whispers in my ear; he pushes my back forward. She caresses my face and ruffles my hair; he shouts and has tantrums like some silverback gorilla with the frustrations of a two-year-old. Like a lover, when they are not around life seems to be missing something. Today there was no gender, he, or she, was a ten-year-old child playing in the forest. Running down slopes, then up hills. Stopping suddenly to look as something in the forest catches their eye. The focused attention only lasting a few second before they are off again, their outstretched hands touching the end of every branch they pass in an endless game of tag. I could hear laughter and calls to come and see what the wind had found. The laughter was infectious and brought a slight smile to my lips as the exuberance made the day more real. Then like an exhausted parent I found a dip on the edge of the lake where I could lie down out of the wind and become an adult once more.

In a drawing class many years ago, I was told only by drawing the spaces could I truly see the object. I found it nonsensical at the time. It seemed like the adolescent argument that a vacuum is something, so how could it be nothing. Over time I have seen I was wrong. Lying on the dried pine needles I was being taught this lesson once more. Looking up to the blue ceiling of sky above me it was the gaps between the branches that created the shapes I could see. They were more modern art than renaissance of course, but still they spoke to me. Organic living blobs, living a quantum life, changing from one shape to another, then back again as the branches extended and return in the wind. A soup of blue protozoan life above me, swirling and pulsating.

Looking round there were other shapes of nothing that revealed something. At the end of my feet was a tree with a great big bite taken out of, like a half-eaten apple core. Beneath it were scatterings of white flakes, like massive toasted almonds slices. The bite in the trunk had regular marks the same size as the giant almond flakes. Teeth marks. It was the work of a beaver. I realised there were other tree stumps scattered around me with conical topes showing the same pattern of teeth. All the bitten trees, and once bitten stumps, were within a meter or two of the lake shore. I saw the scene in front of me differently now. More like an abandoned city with fallen statues and half-finished projects. No sign of the people that once built them. I scanned the water hoping to find a furry face staring back at me. No joy. A slight feeling of guilt came over me. Here was I stretched out in the sun and shade surrounded by evidence of work and industry. If one could say that beavers sweated and toiled, then this was the place they did it. The only sweat on me was where the sun was kissing parts of my skin. As for toil, firstly I am not really sure exactly what toil is? My image of someone toiling is of body bent over, weighed down by the weight of the work they do. Be it bent over a desk or bent over a shovel in a field. That being the case there is no way my long, stretched out, body could qualify as a body toiling. If the beavers were ever to form some socialist party, then based on my current repose I would be one of the early victims of their social revolution. Should this happen, would it by inappropriate to refer to these Bolshevik rodents as 'those dam beavers'?

Beavers are always portrayed in films as kind souls. Industrious in work but also in generosity. Other Norwegian animals do not have such good publicists. I am told on a few occasions' wolves have been seen in the wider vicinity of Oslo. The wolf in Norway seems more divisive than Brexit in the UK. The descendants of Red Riding Hood still hold a grudge against the attempt on Grandma's life. On the other side an unlikely mix of subscribers to the Nature Channel and heavy metal aficionados champion the wolf. For them it represents the true spirit of wild nature and god like forest ghosts. I decide this is not something worth thinking further about, unless of course a wolf were to appear, but I probably wouldn't even know it was there.

I am back on the path. There is an echo to the crunch of my shoes. The echo gets louder but the delay between my feet and the echo reaching my ears gets longer! I am starting to question the laws of physics. Rounding the corner my reality is restored. A man with a rucksack, outdoor clothing and walking shoes. Yes, I know, walking shoes is a silly name, all shoes are for walking in. Now Norwegians are people who respect your space. Your business is your business. If something needs saying they will say it, but only if it needs saying. I am English. Previously I lived in a small English village. We also respect people's right to privacy but unlike Norwegians we have a whole series of words we are required to use to enforce this. Its fine in a crowd to ignore people, but when an Englishman on his own

meets another person on their own, the expectation is to acknowledge them. It may just be a jolly
'Hello', or a stating of the obvious 'Great weather'.
Possibly a slightly more formal 'Good Morning'.
However, silence is rude. The impending meeting
was a clash of two cultures. Should I respect the local culture and stay silent, or stay loyal to my roots
and acknowledge this passing of two strangers? As
we got closer my heart rate increased with the social pressure. Scenarios were being played out in my
head. Could a gesture with no words work? A touch
to my forehead, a wave of my hat, a cheerful smile.
Or would that ruin his day as much as my silence
would ruin my mood. As a child waiting for immun-
isation injections from the school nurse I was always at the front of the line. If it is inevitable, then
get past it as fast as possible. It was a philosophy
that has stood me well over the years, and so my
footsteps increased in tempo as I accelerated my
walk. He looked up. A single glance to me, then back
to inspecting the stones on the path with renewed
interest. You can pick your choice of expression at
this point, 'red rag to a bull', 'stirring up a hornet's
nest', but whichever you select it all reflected the
fact I now felt slightly insulted. Was he really going
to ignore me and a thousand years of British culture? This is how wars start. Two people both believing they are doing the right thing. Cultural diversity is great for a holiday brochure but can be
dangerous in real life. I deaccelerated to give him a
chance to change his mind. This also allowed my

blood pressure to reduce slightly and my rational side to reassert itself. With rationality came wisdom. At 3 meters my eyes locked to his head ready to fire my verbal missile. "Hi-Hi" I sung out. The traditional Norwegian greeting I used on entering a shop. My standards were upheld, but I had reached out to use his culture rather than mine. He looked up. "Good morning" he said in a wonderful plum English accent.

We both looked a little shameful. Statistically speaking we were both right to expect the other to be Norwegian. I understood now why some people wear union jack t-shirts or shorts. Its helps life. Announce who you are to the world and let them treat you accordingly.

The pressure from this short meeting was too much for me. A small side path appeared, and I took it in the belief there was less chance to meet another walker on it. The path was narrower and covered with soft pine needles. It was like leaving a party and stepping out into sudden silence. Not real silence. There isn't a word for it. It's the opposite of deafened. Un-deafened? The carpet of pine needles on soil removed the sound of my movement. The ground became softer on my feet giving more spring to my steps. I was the wolf walking silently through the forest. I was a walking audio black hole. Sound could reach my ears and be absorbed, but no sound was given out. I was a stealth walker, off grid and off radar. It was also darker. The narrow path weaved between small gaps in the trees. Bark, leaves and branches were all much closer to my face. Sometimes I was forced to duck and swerve. My silent approach and the natural cover meant I started to surprise animals going about their business. Plenty of fieldfares made a rapid departure, calling out to warn others that the wolf was in the forest. A red squirrel on a branch stopped his arboreal searching to stare at me in curiosity. Did humans never come this far into the forest? I assumed not. He just returned to his search having decided I was no threat. The dark red tail twitching as he moved over and under branches. An insatiable curiosity to explore everything at every height and every angle. He disappeared with a sudden, seemingly impossible jump.

Just as the big gravel path had been a path of dominance, so I was now on a path of submission. The old path reflected modern human life. It went where it wanted to go. It removed obstacles. It smoothed out irregularities. It changed the texture of the ground beneath it. My current path had to go where the forest made it. Obstacles like trees and rocks had to be gone around. If a distance was 20 meters as the crow flies it was 50 meters as the wolf walks. Small dips and rises were traversed. Larger ones required irregular arcs to get around. Every 20 steps I would change direction slightly, like a sailing boat in an irregular squall. The path kept fighting the terrain to get back on course. And the terrain kept pushing it away, up, down, left, right, but never flat and forward. It was tiring work. Most of the time I had to watch where my feet were going to avoid tree roots and other traps. Short glances up were all I could allow myself, and because of this I lost all sense of direction. All the tricks from the books were no use. Look at the shadows, but the shadows were few and my watch said it was close to midday when the sun was unhelpfully overhead. Moss grows on north side of a tree, well maybe in the open but certainly not in the middle of a dark forest where sunlight is not there to dry out the south facing moss. I had entered the Bermuda triangle of Norwegian forests. Every direction was north. At a time like this there are only two choices. The path you have travelled to get there is like a long piece of string that can take you back out to the safety of where you entered the forest. Or you can go forward in ignorance of the outcome. Deciding you are too committed to your path to turn back. Norway is a big country. I tried to work out how far I might go before hitting another road or man-made path. Might I reach the arctic circle and find myself walking out of the trees into a landscape of icebergs and reindeer? Of course not, the trees stop before the arctic circle. Anyway, I would be dead long before I got there. Not knowing works two ways. I also told myself that the end of the path could be around the next corner, over the next peak. I was an investor with a sinking stock. Should I sell it now and take the loss or hang on in the belief it will rebound. Psychologists will tell you people value what they own more than what they could own. So it was with my path. It was my path. I was committed to it. The cost of giving it up seemed too great for my pride to bear. I carried on.

At this point, knowing I was lost actually helped. I didn't have to lie to myself that I knew what I was doing. It was easy to know what I had to do. Just keep walking as far and as fast as possible. My pace picked up. The wolf had become a Zulu warrior. I had read the books and seen the films. The Zulu warriors could travel great distance at speed and then still fight a battle. They would sing and focus their minds in a meditative way, enabling them to live in the moment and ignore the pain from their exhausted bodies. I searched for a song to sing. "You're in the mood for a dance.. and when you get the chance...". Why Dancing Queen from Abba I have no idea. Once you start Dancing Queen it is hard to get it out of your head. I got more confident in my singing. I wasn't sure they were the right words, but they rhymed and made sense for my memory of the song. Ten minutes later I had exhausted Dancing Queen and searched for a replacement. The Abba theme continued "I work all day, I work all night". It deviated slightly "I'm always looking for a fight" but I got to the chorus and was back on track "Money, Money, Money". On the third money I turned a corner to find a clearing with two women staring in my direction. I was embarrassed to be caught singing. I then became more embarrassed, as I realised, they both were topless. Sunbathing in this oasis of sunshine. They were not embarrassed. Clearly not English. One of them cheerfully said something in Norwegian to me. "Sorry I am English". Another smile from them and a change of language "Are you trying to leave Europe?" she asked. The great thing about Norwegians is they have a similar sense of humour to the British. Irony, sarcasm, wit are all things they understand, and we share between our nations. "I need a way back to civilisation please". They pointed to a gap in the clearing "About 5 minutes' walk that way". "Thank you" and I strode off.

They were right, and five minutes later I was back on the noisy gravel. I made what I considered to be an intelligent, yet uninformed, decision and chose to head left rather than right. Time would show that going left was the right choice. It was not clear to me where I had appeared. Like the Terminator arriving in a new time I had to take my bearings and look for evidence of where I had arrived. I was pretty sure the year was still the same. But where was I?

THE FAT MAN

He walks slowly into the café. It's a rolling walk, moving the bulk of his body from left, to right, back to left. Without this shift of weight to free each leg he might have become a great oak tree, rooted to one spot for life. It's a gentle movement, even attractive. There is no hurry in it, no urgency. The steps are small. His centre of gravity never strays far from the middle of his torso. Just like the mighty oak tree, I would not want to be close to him in a windstorm, for fear of being crushed as a mighty sudden gust catches him off guard. Here in the café, he is safe from the elements that might conspire to topple him. There are obstacles to be manoeuvred past. Chair backs creating valleys and canyons, just wide enough for the average person to flow through. Clearly, he is a master of these rapids, he turns sideways to roll through, his body turning left and right. It's a graceful walk with rhythm. I can see an invisible dance partner with him sliding round his body as he passes each chair.

His lower legs are like mine. He even has the same skinny jeans around them. As my eyes go up the leg the shape of the oak tree starts to form. On a good day I might call myself a Cyprus tree. Very vertical. Most of my branches heading up in search of the sun. His branches are more horizontal, keeping his legs in permanent shadow. Where do you get trousers with a larger waist than leg size? Would that belt go twice round my waist? I have nastier thoughts. I would not want to sit next to him on an aeroplane flight. His face is kind, I like it, but that body would invade my already small personal space like a vertical mattress confining one side of my body. A wall of flesh. Would he even feel my elbows digging into him? What if he had a heart attack on the flight, would I ever be able to call for help? He is very fat. Is it his fault or is he just a product of the diversity of nature?

He has reached the counter. His body finally stops. Put him in a red outfit and from behind I would think Santa Claus had arrived to get his caffeine before a busy night. The barista looks expectantly at him. Some of them are students, young faces, earning cash to travel and enjoy life. She is not one of them. She is there to keep her family. Her shampoo does not give an expensive glow to her hair. I suspect she was up earlier than me, making lunch boxes, putting on laundry before coming out to create expensive indulgences for people with less burden in their life. It seems improbable that she would ever pay this much for a coffee.

He is looking along the menus on the wall above her. No eye contact is made yet. I think he is using the menus as a way to pause and catch his breath, before having to talk. Finally, he looks down and orders a coffee – he would have known he was having that. She asks him is he would like any caramel in his coffee. Then she asks if he would like to take advantage of the special offer on bacon rolls. Around them posters of giant cake say things like 'spoil yourself' and 'you deserve it'. It is just business. No one wants to make him fatter; they just want him to buy more. Teams of suits and high heel shoes toiling in windowless rooms, inventing ways to make people spend more. Creating meal deals, buy one get one half price, loyalty programs that reward you for spending more. He wasn't strong enough to avoid coming in, but like Christ, he manages to resist the temptations others put in front of him. He sticks with just coffee. I like him more.

There is a small, slate blue bag, on a strap over his shoulder. Some would call it a man-bag. For some reason they are always very small when carried by overweight men, and rather larger when carried by skinny men. The forces of irony at work. Would a therapist say they represented how the person wants to be? Or do skinny men just need to carry more stuff like jumpers to keep warm. He took out a wallet, then from inside the wallet a card, then another card. The first showed his loyalty to the café chain. There wasn't another coffee stop on this road for 10 miles, so loyalty might be the wrong word. Should it be called a relationship card. Tell us about yourself, where you live, where you travel to, do you have a sweet tooth, do you crave the status of a large latte, or is fiscal prudence more your character resisting every opportunity we offer to get a larger drink for a little bit more of your money. As she electronically scanned his loyalty card, I imagined the chain of event that followed. Electricity was used to send the information to headquarters. Numbers were recalculated – his loyalty points to date, the average spend for his demographic, correlation coefficients to estimate what others like him normally buy with their coffee, a text message automatically generated back to his phone offering 50% off a chocolate brownie slice with his next visit. As he returned the cards to their dark home in his bag, I heard the Bing of a text message arriving on his phone. The chain was complete. The bait was set for his next visit.

He moved to one side, joining the other loiters impatient for their coffee to be ready. Some tapping on their phone screens. Two women chatting, catching up on their children's development at school and summer holiday plans. He looked happy in the crowd. There were other men with bellies. Like a range of pregnant men – one was about 3 months, another probably 7 months judging by the pressure against his shirt. Overweight men could learn something from women's pregnancy clothing ranges. How to better hide the bump, and never, never, wear horizontal stripes.

"Skinny latte for Charles"

He moved forward to take it. I had not figured him for a Charles. Do people call him Charlie?

Charles is so formal. Fat people are meant to be jolly. Charlie made more sense. Why are fat people meant to be jolly? I can't see a reason they should be any more jolly than other size people. Not if its real. I guess if you believe overweight and insecurity go together then it could be some form of compensation behaviour. Like the woman who laughs too much on a date, the insecure person who appears jolly in public. It's stupid. I know overweight people who are happy, and others who have not yet found happiness. I think it's a stereotype from films. When no one wanted to acknowledge black people having rights they appeared in films as happy with their role in life. Put down but happy, so not a problem. Maybe fat people are the new black people? We see them, we know they will have a shorter life, we realise however uncomfortable our airline seat is it must be worse for them but resent them sitting next to us, we know they will not be the hero in the movie, but we are happy to think they are okay with that and we don't need to help them. I feel a bit better knowing that I also discriminate against skinny people. The girls I look at and think should be rushed to a restaurant. The men I think must have AIDS because no one could be that thin normally. We like average people.

Charles scans the room. I imagine he is looking at the empty chairs and the judging routes to get to them. He goes for an upright chair one row back. Safe in the crowd but not a challenge to get to. My coffee has gone cold, and I need to be back on the road. Charles is scanning the room. He watches as a black man in a smart blue business suit comes in. I stand up. I send a look to Charles, as if to say it's your turn now to watch and judge the room. Be kinder than me.

THE JOURNEY

The sun is behind me. In front of me is darkness. My shadow starts from my feet but slowly dissolves away. The only thing that can kill a shadow is darkness. So dark it absorbs everything. A sun behind me, a black hole in front. There is an arch of pink around the darkness. Its smooth pink like a well-worn limestone sculpted by years of wind. I can feel the wind. It's not natural. It's too regular. It has a rhythm to it. It buffets me from behind, blowing my hair forward, pushing me towards the darkness. All this happens in a second or two, then it relaxes and changes direction. It builds once more, but this time coming from in front of me, blowing my hair backwards to reveal my face once more. This repeats, again, and again, and again. Its predictable but its unnerving. It makes everything complex. If I lit a candle my hand would be perpetually circling the flickering flame to keep it alive. I get flashes of vision as my hair covers my face, then clears, only to be obstructed once more. My whole body feels this wind as my clothing pushes against my skin. It's not a cold wind. More like an approaching storm. It has warmth and moisture. A parasitic plant with strong roots would thrive in it, stealing water, spreading its seeds. The wind has a voice. It's a low frequency sound. It comes from in front not behind. There is some sort of life in the darkness ahead. Not traditional life. It feels bigger than whale. More experienced of life than a redwood tree. Its large, and its alive, but it is not anything you would find in an encyclopaedia of life. It's like a super organism lives in the darkness. Or makes the darkness.

I pull out a head torch. It takes me a whole minute to get it on. I need to catch the wind when it blows my hair back. I keep missing the timing. The elastic head band keeps trapping my hair at the wrong time, making me blind. I concentrate. Like someone getting to the end of an escalator and planning their first step off. Finally, I get the timing right. My hair is held behind my face and I get to see better. Not perfect, but not blind. It's not a powerful head torch. Both the bright light behind and the darkness in front can defeat it. It works best on the surface of the pink arch, creating Tinkerbell like patterns as my head moves. I take five steps forward.

Five small steps. That's about the length of my body if I was lying down. It enough to take me into near darkness. The pink entrance arch is behind me. The sunshine has surrendered. Darkness is welcoming me. Shaking my hand, putting its arm round me, pulling me in. The wind whispers in my ear 'Pleased to meet you', 'Make yourself at home', 'it's perfectly safe'. Then as it changes direction, it whispers 'People don't live in darkness', 'Don't be a fool', 'Run'.

I let the devil and the angel argue for my soul as my
eye pupils enlarge to take in any light they can find.
The head torch starts to become more useful. I have
a vision of a fried egg in front of me. A core beam
of yellow light, then a gentle white ring of diffuse
light around it. There is no edge to it. It just becomes
darkness, but I can't exactly tell where that tran-
sition happens. I feel like a cyclops. I should have
brought another torch. Two eyes are better than
one. I edge forward.

Something is touching my arm. Not holding it,
just brushing against it. I am very still. Below my
neck nothing moves. My head turns. It looks like a
rope, or maybe a vine. It's not regularly enough to
be manmade, so not a rope. My head follows it up to
find its source. Nothing is very clear. In the glow it
looks like there is a roof above me. It's not flat roof
and it has a luminous pink glow to it. Like the arch,
but whiter. It could just be a pattern on my eyes,
but I think it's real. The vine is attached, a sort of
plant like stalactite growing down. It moves in the
wind, but only a little. My fingers appear in the light
as I reach out to touch it. The texture is smooth
to touch. Its firmer and give good resistance to the
wind. My touch moves it a little, but like the wind
I can't move it very far. It is not rigid, but it has ri-
gidity, like an English longbow. There are more of
them. In the gloom I see a pattern of vertical lines
around me. All of them secured from above, none of
them reaching the floor. The torch light makes them
visible like a dark watercolour of a sparse upside-

down crop in bad moonlight. There is not enough of them to block my way. In fact, I take comfort in them, like a bannister on a staircase.

As I walk forward the floor starts to incline gently uphill. My heart rate is settling down as I focus on finding a path forward. I need a name for the vertical vine things. If I was telling someone about them, they would need a name. It seems silly right now but it's important to me. From time to time I am steadying myself by grabbing them. I want to know what to call them. Stalactites? Tendrils? Something made up – Voliphant, Bowfeet, Danglebots? The last one sounds good, like some invented word in Harry Potter. Neither fearsome, nor loving. A Danglebot just is what it is. It gets steeper and I grab a Danglebot in each hand to pull myself forward. I try to time my steps with the blasts of wind from behind me to push me further with each step. After a minute I reach the peak. The floor suddenly levels. Worryingly the Danglebots stop at this point, as if they know to go no further.

The floor seems more organic now. Not organic as in chemistry, or organic as in environmentally friendly farming. How both of them use the same word but mean such different things is beyond me? Rather organic as in softer, mushier, damper – like a compost heap feels more organic than a pebble beach. There is an aroma. A slight squelch under foot. It's the only noise apart from the wind. My footsteps become smaller. Squelchy also means slippery. The incline is rapidly changing to downhill and there are no Danglebots to hold on to. The tunnel must be widening out – or my batteries are running down, because I can't see any walls above me or to either side. I edge further forward, then my feet give way sliding from under me. I know I am falling. Not just falling to the ground but falling into a hole or a crevasse. I am vertical but falling, my back bumping against the floor that has become a wall behind me. Every so often a soft obstacle hits me and changes my orientation slightly, but still the direction is down. I pick up speed. The only wind now is air rushing past me as I accelerate down. I land with a hard, stinging, splash.

It's not water. The viscosity is higher, it seems denser, and stickier. The landing knocked the air out of my body, like an egg breaking and losing its yolk. My chest and lungs are working hard to replace the lost oxygen. Large breaths with more breathing in than out. Reflating my body, but it's not oxygen. There is oxygen in it, along with some cocktail of noxious gases, the black sheep of the oxygen family. As my breath comes back, I start trying to hold my breath longer to stop the stench refreshing itself every time air comes into me. I am floating higher than I would in water. I feel like a seal with its head raised up out of the sea. There are lumps in whatever sea of liquid I am in. More like a swamp or a soup than a drink. My feet and arms are paddling. They hit different materials. All wet, some hard, some soft. A few more breaths and I am feeling dizzy. The head torch is still working and its casting long shadows on the surface of the sea as its beam catches lumps floating in the water. The dizziness gets stronger and with it my eyes start to blur. Everything goes dark, but the torch is still on. I pass out from the fumes.

My eyes are open, I know my hand is in front of my face, but I see nothing. I wiggle my fingers, still nothing. How do you know you are seeing properly when you see nothing but blackness? Do blind people think their eyes are open when they see nothing? It feels like there are a hundred hands all round my body. Every part of me feels as if fingers are gently stroking me, like hundred amateur pickpockets searching through my clothing. It's warm. There is no wind, but there is noise. Creaking sounds like a sailing ship mixed with various types of growling. Deep growling like distant thunder. Higher regular growling, maybe a distant scared dog. The sounds come from all around me and the hundred hands seem to be pushing me slowly in a direction I can feel but cannot see. I don't jump any more from a strange touch, there are so many of them. In fact, they become comforting, with each ripple they relax me more. Is this what a massage in a sensory deprivation tank would feel like? There are no points or edges, just surfaces and pressures. There is so little to be certain of anymore. I don't know where I am, or where this gentle current is taking me. I am not sure if I am blind, or how I am managing to be alive even. Am I alive? Can there be reality when you are wrapped in warm total darkness. There is no hot or cold, no peaks or troughs. The sounds are random and come from all directions. They are the only unpredictable thing in this constant world. One other thing is changing. Not randomly. It's the pressure on my body which is getting stronger. It subtle but it clearly discernible. Its compressing everything. The gentle hands are pushing up against me. I am becoming a mummy unable to move my limbs. My body becomes more ridged with the pressure. The pressure now coming in waves. At the peak of each wave I am forced to breath out, like a wet cloth being wrung dry.

There is a pause. The pressure is strong and constant, its physical strength creates a mental pressure in my mind. For some reason I imagine myself as one of an army of infantry waiting for a command. Or an inflated balloon waiting for a pin. Maybe we are on a precipice. In this world I could be anywhere and not know it. I can't prepare for whatever is going to happen because I have no information about where I am or what's around me. Then the order goes out. A massive wave of pressure builds up and me and everything around me moves forward as one unified object. We are squeezed through some sort of bottle neck, then everything changes. In a second my blindness has gone only to be replaced by such strong white light that I close my eyes unable to bear the pain. Everything is dropping away from me. The hands, the warmth, they are all evaporating. My bare skin suddenly can feel temperature changes. It's getting colder. Drops of liquid are running down the back of my neck. I can open my eyes a little. My clothes are all damp, but not wet. Brown patches on them suggest I may have been cross country running across a mudflat in a rainstorm. I thank the gods of fate that I don't have a mirror and there is no one to see me like this, but I have pride on my face. A pride from having made it through. I went in and I came out. I can tell you what it's like but not what happened to me. Which is better than knowing what happened but being unable to tell you what it was like.

Printed in Great Britain
by Amazon